This book is entirely a work of fiction. The names, characters, and incidents portrayed in it are the work of the author's imagination. Any resemblance to actual persons, living or dead, events or localities is entirely coincidental.

www.onetruekev.co.uk

This paperback edition 2024

A catalogue record for this book is available from the British Library

ISBN: 978-1-7385396-1-1

For Helen

Thank you for all your encouragement and support

January

1st January

Resolution

With a pounding head he opened his eyes, and looked around. He'd made it as far as the sofa last night, and there was a trail of clothes leading back to the front door.

He staggered to the kitchen and opened the fridge. There was no Pepsi, in fact there were no fizzy drinks at all, only water and milk.

He opened the cupboard, and all the chocolate and biscuits had gone. He couldn't believe he had polished off all of them last night.

He phone bleeped.

The text read, "Good luck with the sugar free New Year's resolution."

Nnooooooooooooo!!!!!

2nd January

Back To Work

It was the first day back after the Christmas holiday period. Eleven days without any work, without having to get up early and do anything.

Her movement was slow, it took soooo much longer to do anything, movement was a chore. It was as if she was sticking to everything, unable to pick her feet up, or move her arms, as if her whole body was a single lump. And it was uncomfortable, her skin was leaking, and she felt slimy, and it was a funny colour.

As normal, the first day back at work and she was feeling slug-ish.

3rd January

Paranormal Activity

Everything the poor girl did was being scrutinised by the whole town. Whenever she was about there were reports of paranormal activity happening. The paranormal activity followed her around wherever she went, and it ended up that people didn't want her anywhere near them or their property anymore.

Wherever she went she heard the whispers, nothing ever to her face, as they were afraid of her. She heard the words though, 'there goes the witch, stay away from her.'

But she was perfectly normal. It wasn't her fault.

It was all me. No one paid any attention to her lackey.

4th January

Charity Shop.

She couldn't help herself, she just couldn't walk past a charity shop without going in and having a look.

There was always the hope that the perfect items of clothing would be there, just waiting for her to come and collect it. It rarely was.

She browsed the bric-a-brac looking for potential presents for her ornament mad parents. Looked at the books, CDs, DVDs and records, and even the toys and games.

Half an hour gone in the blink of an eye, and she wandered to the till with numerous items she didn't need, or remember picking up.

£4.68 please.

5th January

Inspiration

He'd gone into the charity shop to search for the normal items, records and books, he didn't usually bother with any other sections, but he hadn't been in this shop before, so took an amble around it.

Then he saw it, just what he needed to be an inspiration to his writing, he picked it up and looked for a price. Wow, it was a bargain at two pounds, so he bought it, and took it home.

She took one look at it sat on the kitchen table.

"What on earth are you going to do with a wooden typewriter?"

6th January

Twelfth Night

"Shall we go for dinner tonight dear?" Asked Mrs Muddle.

"What about taking the decorations down dear, it's twelfth night," Replied Mr Muddle.

"That's alright, we can do it when we get back from the meal."

As the meal dragged on, Mrs Muddle asked, "Would you like another drink darling?"

"Sounds good to me."

Many drinks later, they headed for home. Too much to eat and drink meant Mr Muddle headed straight for bed. The next morning he woke up to find the decorations still up.

"Oh dear," said a grinning Mrs Muddle, "They'll have to stay up all year."

7th January

A Change Of View

When he started out his political campaigning he was considered as a new breed of radical to the far left of the spectrum. But over the long span of his political career, it appeared that his views were becoming a lot less and less radical. They became considered as more commonplace, more middle of the road as he aged. But as time went by so how his views were considered changed again, and now they were considered to be radical again.

But to his utter dismay his views were now considered to be at the far right of the spectrum.

8th January

Waiting

He'd been waiting patiently for quite some time now, he'd found a chair to sit on, and was watching and listening for his number to come up. He wasn't in any rush, there was no need to be. He didn't understand why some people found it necessary to push in, and harangue those behind the counter because their number hadn't been called yet.

Everyone seemed in such a rush nowadays, instant gratification was the thing. He didn't care, he knew his number would come up eventually, and when it did he will have the complete set of happy meal toys.

9th January

Running

Every day for the last six months the alarm had gone off at the same time; six in the morning, and he'd got out of bed, put on his kit and gone out for a run. He had average over six kilometres each morning, racking up over one thousand so far since he had started running.

He'd lost six stone in weight, and was now in clothes four sizes smaller, he was the fittest he had been since school.

Everyone was happy for him, except himself. He still felt miserable, nothing could change that for him.

Except, possibly, that bus.

10th January

Life And Soul

He thought he was a funny man. He thought he was the life and soul of the party. He thought he was being sociable and friendly. These were the superpowers he believed he had when he was out drinking. That drinking changed the introverted him into an extrovert version of him that everyone thought was a great guy.

But he was blind to the truth. They didn't even like him, they only just about tolerated him, whispering behind his back.

In reality he was just being a dick and had turned into a full blown alcoholic and he didn't know.

11th January

Crossing

The chicken had crossed the road, rolled in the mud and crossed back again, and was delighted about being a dirty double crosser.

The turkey was jealous of the chicken, it had been after the road crossing job for years, and to be pecked at the post by the chicken was the last straw.

The fox had been tipped off, he'd been given the time and place of the crossing and was in hiding, waiting.

The chicken had the day off, and the turkey was given a trial, for holiday cover.

The turkey, so pleased, had forgotten about the fox.

12th January

The Punch

Suddenly a fist flies over the left shoulder of the man in front of me. Thrown by one of his friends, I've been blindsided by the man in my face. The punch catches me on the lips, I know I've been hit, but my head doesn't move, I barely feel the contact.

I taste the blood in my mouth; the strong metallic taste is now all that is there, pushing away the beer taste that was there before. I assume I must be cut on the inside of my mouth, from where the lips have been crushed against my teeth.

13th January

A Little Bit Of Rain

It had started raining quite heavily when he pulled into the car park, there were a few spaces right next to one of the walkways that were empty, so he parked quite happily in one of them, as being next to the walkway he could be out of the rain in a few seconds, he couldn't believe that others were parking further away.

When he got back to the car an hour later he knew why; they had local knowledge, the space he'd been happy to park in was now a small lake, he'd have to paddle to his car.

14th January

A Nice Wool Mix

I had been thinking about getting a pet, but I was looking at getting something different, I had narrowed it down, but asked my friend Ellie what I should do.

"Which do you think would be better to get as a pet? A kangaroo or a sheep?"

Without a pause, Ellie responded,

"Get both."

"Why would I want both?"

"Well they would always keep you warm in winter."

"How do you work that out?"

"It's obvious really, get one of each and breed the two together, because when you mix a kangaroo and a sheep you get a woolly jumper!"

15th January

Angry Man

The man is shouting at me, I see his mouth moving and the hateful look on his face, but I can't make out what he is saying. Part of this is because of my drunkenness, but also because of his drunkenness, making his words a bit nonsensical.

However the loud music coming from all around, is what is stopping the shouting getting through, it's difficult to hear anything over the music. Cameo's "Word Up", and it's all I can do not to sing, but I doubt it will help the mood of the angry red-faced man in front of me.

16th January

Foodman

With bananas for hands, and mushrooms for feet. A cauliflower for a brain in a head made of beet.

Artichoke as a heart, and lungs that were pears. Arms of celery reached for the spaghetti styled hair.

Carrot for a nose and Brussel sprouts for eyes looked at turnips for knees and leek made thighs.

Sweet potato filled torso half stuffed with rice, peanuts for teeth surrounded a tongue made of ice.

Marrows for calves and a pumpkin behind. Rosemary and sage instead of a mind.

What once was a man had completely changed, into a vegetarian's pantry well rearranged.

17th January

The Charlatan

In the middle of the crowded bar, just as there was a sudden pause in the constant buzz of conversation, there was one loud strident voice heard.

“I'm a Charlatan” a man blurted out. A few of the people crammed into the bar looked over in his direction. Not one of them seemed to care whether the man was a Charlatan or not, none of them knew him.

Then, less than a couple of seconds later there was a loud Mancunian voice shouting back. The Charlatans were shite, you would have been better off saying you were a Happy Monday.

18th January

Speak Up

Have you ever noticed the tendency for old people to get louder and louder as they speak, and the fact that they have absolutely no filter on what comes out of their mouths?

You can be having a normal everyday conversation, at a volume that only those having the conversation can hear, when bit by bit as they turn the direction of the conversation to something that makes a younger generation cringe at the casual racism of it, the volume increases, and then that moment comes; when everyone else for a twenty yard radius goes quiet, as the pensioners shout!

19th January

Clive

There was an elephant called Clive. He was friends with a chicken called Jeminah.

One day they had an argument. No one knows how it started, they called each other names, getting madder as the argument proceeded. Clive used his trunk and squirted Jeminah with water. Jeminah retaliated by rushing up to Clive and pecking him.

Clive felt the slight sting of the pecking and was annoyed. He waited until Jeminah stopped pecking and then stamped on her.

The argument was over and the vultures had something to eat.

Clive moved on and became friends with a hyena called Trevor.

20th January

Lost Gardens

Today's trip was to the Lost Gardens of Heligan, now my original response, besides who cares about gardens, was if they are lost, how are we going to find them, and why would we bother?

Apparently they aren't that lost. They have sign posts directing you to them from miles away. Not only that, but we certainly weren't the only people to find them today.

Overflow car parking was in full effect, we were almost back in Devon by the time we got parked. Thousands of people had found the lost gardens.

They would be rubbish at hide and seek.

21st January

The Stirrer

Jim liked to stir the pot, as he called it. He liked to make it as murky as he possible could so that it obfuscated the important issues of the day.

He delighted in the confusion he though it brought about, he believed that it added a certain mystery to his aura, and that having this air of mystery about him made people interesting in him.

But what Jim didn't realise is that all the obfuscation did was enable people to see right through him and his 'mysterious' persona and realise that he was nothing more than a shit stirrer.

22nd January

Hidden Unicorns

Everybody thought that they had been wiped out. That the unicorns were nothing but a myth, a story for children. But as it turned out they weren't. The unicorns were real, they had only gone into deep cover. They morphed into being Rhinos and Narwhals so that they could live in peace away from the human's prying eyes as they waited for their time.

For more than six millennia they hid themselves away, but the time for them to make their comeback was nigh. They were coming back and going to take over the world and imprison all the humans.

23rd January

After The Interview

The interview had gone as well as she could have expected. The hard work preparing had paid off, she had answers to all the questions that they had asked, there was only the one area where the interviewer seemed to have an issue, and that was around the engagement with senior stakeholders. For some reason they appeared to want years of experience in doing this, despite the fact it was for an entry level role.

She could only wait now; they would let her know either way soon.

It was sooner than expected; she got the job the next day.

24th January

Sky Go

I really don't understand what use Sky Go is, I've tried to use it a few times, it won't work at all on either of my usual browsers, and when I put the details in to IE it says it doesn't work on the current version, so brings up a window from medieval times.

It doesn't allow access from the work wi-fi, saying it's a corporate network, and it doesn't work whilst on holiday in the UK, saying the hotel's wi-fi is corporate.

Sky Go my arse, more like Sky stay at home where you can see the TV anyway.

25th January

Animal Cruelty

"Mummy, we have to stop them," cried little Jessica,

"Stop who darling?"

"The men torturing those animals, the ones that sound seriously in pain."

Jessica's mum looked around, but failed to spot any animals, so she asked "What animals, sweetheart?"

"Those!" Jessica shouted as she pointed them out, "The ones that those men in skirts have got in their arms, can't you hear the horrible screeching the poor animals are making?"

Jessica's mum laughed, "Darling, they aren't animals, they are called bagpipes, they are traditional Scottish musical instruments."

Jessica didn't seem to agree, "Musical instruments? You could have fooled me."

26th January

Latency

The whole of the courtroom was shocked when the prosecution barrister left the ground and started to float up to the ceiling. All the while he did so he struggled against the unseen force lifting him up there, arms flailing and high sotto voice crying out in shock and surprise.

But the system had pushed me too far this time. If they were going to try and put me in prison for something I was no part of, then I would go down fighting.

For too long I had ignored the ancient power lying latent within me. But no longer.

27th January

Queue Jumper

The woman had two items in her hand, a box of tissues, and a box of ibuprofen. They only had two tills open again, always the same at this time in the morning.

She looked around the corner and the queue was up the aisle. She didn't go to the end of the queue, she stood in front of a trolley glaring at the man leaning on it.

He wasn't paying her any attention at first, but he eventually noticed her and uttered the words she wanted to hear.

"You can go in front of me."

She didn't say thanks.

28th January

The Dark

How long have I been stuck in here now? Hours? Days perhaps? Weeks even? It's darker than anything I have ever known before, I can't see a thing, not even my hand an inch in front of my nose, not even the supposedly luminous hands on my watch. I have no idea of the time or date. I can't even sit up in here, only turn over.

This has gone on for too long, surely. It was only supposed to be a temporary hiding place for me until things blew over. Are they ever going to come and disinter me?

29th January

One Last Putt

Bill Turner walked up the 18th fairway to the last green. He had played the most magnificent tournament of golf possible. He was eight shots clear of the rest of the field in his very first professional tournament.

No one had ever heard of him before this, and now here he was, lining up his eight foot putt to win the million dollar purse and secure the life for himself and his family.

Only for that to be the time when the dreaded yips would start. Instead of a win with one putt, he ten putted and lost the lot.

30th January

Adigia Leaves

The two youngsters had spent every day of their young lives doing exactly the same thing. They'd come out into the forest to find some Adigia leaves for them to chew during the day. There were always plenty of the bitter leaves growing in the shadow of the trees. They didn't like the taste, and only did it because they were told to.

What they didn't know it was their parents' way to obviate their need for any other food. They didn't know that they were hungry and that the bitter leaves was the only way to feed them.

31st January

The New Queen

I had been crowned as the Queen with the full ceremony that went with it. The princess had been exiled in childhood, sent away from the castle when only young, the princess that was sent away was now recalled to rule when her father had gone mad and was unable to do so himself. With no other children, there was only her left to be the ruler.

But I am not the Princess. I am an usurper, my best friend, the real princess had died when she drowned in the lake. I had taken her clothes, and no one noticed.

February

1st February

The Earthquake

Everything around them was a hive of kinetic energy. The people, the animals, the plants, and even the buildings were all in motion.

There was nothing that was still.

Except the old man.

He didn't move a muscle sat in his chair as the earthquake caused havoc with the world. No one paid any attention to him as they were all too busy running from the chaos of their collapsing world.

Not one single person realised that it was the old man who was causing the earthquake. That he had seen enough of man's cruelty and was ending it all.

2nd February

Performing Monkey

One day the performing monkey fell out of the tree.

Gasps, "Why did the monkey fall out of the tree?"

A shout, "Because it's dead."

No one believed this, but as the minutes passed there was no movement from the monkey. After a couple of hours someone from the crowd approached the prostrate monkey and confirmed what was feared, it was dead.

The crowd started to disperse, and as they did someone was heard to say, "That wasn't the best trick to finish with was it? What's the monkey going to do for an encore?"

Some people are never happy.

3rd February

Uncontactable

When he'd said to them at work that where he was going on holiday in Cornwall would have no signal, so they wouldn't be able to contact him about the project cutover at the weekend, he'd said it as a tongue in cheek comment.

On arrival at the lodge at the end of a country lane that had only been found via overgrown roads narrower than his tie, he took out his phone to see if there were any messages, only to see the words "No Service" on it.

He really was going to be out of contact all week.

4th February

Distracted

He was under pressure, there were a great deal of people depending on his leadership, and yet here he was sat in this small cottage, in effect hiding.

So much was going through his mind about what he needed to do, how he could organise his people, and what he needed to win the day.

Yet there was something nagging at him, something that he had to do here and now, an immediate concern for him to see to, yet he couldn't remember what.

A funny smell was distracting him, and a voice yelled.

"Alfred, you're burning the cakes again!"

5th February

Collecting

No one cared how many records he had, they're all too busy with their own lives and interests to listen to him talking about his collection, let alone to waste time by going round to look at them all.

It was taking over his life. There wasn't really any more space in the house for more records, not without it becoming a health and safety issue.

He had to stop buying records, and look at sorting out and selling some to get some space back.

His phone beeped with a message.

"Auction ending soon"

He pressed the bid now button.

6th February

Snore Wars

"How did you sleep?"

"Not well, it was too dark, and you were snoring really loudly."

"That's strange, when I woke up you were fast asleep and the snoring coming from you was loud enough to wake the dead if they were asleep."

"Did it wake you up?"

"No."

"Well you're not dead and it didn't wake you, so how'd it manage to wake the dead, or was it just that you couldn't hear me because you were snoring louder than me?"

"You were both snoring like you were calling whales home, no wonder there are some beached at Padstow."

7th February

The Dissertation

Group two, your dissertation subject is "Secret Trusts – what are they and how are they applied?"

6000 words to be in by the end of April.

She sat there on the verge of tears. No one else in group two had English as their first language, not even the tutor. The vagaries of alphabetised groupings had done her in again. No one she could talk to about it, and 6000 words on secret trusts?

Someone was taking the piss, there's a hint and a half in the title. No one knew anything about them, they were secret!!

A fail beckoned.

8th February

Device Not Recognised

Device not recognised!

What do you mean device not recognised? How would the machine know that there was a device there not to be recognised if it hadn't recognised there was a device there in the first place?

Especially when it tells you which USB port the unrecognised device is attached to. And then it tells you what type of device it is that is unrecognised.

The device shows up in explorer and can be used as it should be, so it turns out it is recognised after all.

The device is unplugged, and the machine says "unrecognised device removed."

9th February

The Keys

“Where are the keys, I can’t find the keys, I know I had them when I left the lodge this morning as we locked up.”

“Are you sure we locked up the lodge? We were already in the car with your parents waiting for your sisters when they left.”

“I know I had the key, it has to be in here somewhere.”

“Why don’t you go in and check there first?”

“NO!! I had the key, I know I did.”

“What are you looking for?”

“The key!”

“Oh, you mean the one you left on the kitchen bench this morning?”

10th February

The Unexpected Parcel

David wasn’t expecting the large parcel on his door-step, he dragged it inside and tore the cardboard from it. It was a large picture, upon seeing the image within the frame, his mouth gaped open; he was rooted to the spot, frightened beyond belief. His bladder let go as the ghosts of his father’s past caught up with him.

The picture was of Pol Pot, disturbing enough by itself, but the speech bubble shaped post-it note in the front of Pol Pot’s mouth made it worse. Upon it were the bold type faced words that said,

“YOU’RE NEXT!”

David fainted.

11th February

12 Men and Women

The twelve men and women sat around the table trying to make a decision. Some made their minds up straight away, others were indecisive, finding the choice in front of them more difficult than it really should be.

Finally, the last of them made up their minds, they could not all agree. They were asked what their decision was, their leader stood up, looking around the table before announcing the outcome from their deliberations.

"We have decided that we shall have seven cups of coffee, four cups of tea, and the awkward one on the end wants an orange juice."

12th February

Inanimate

He opened his eyes, but there was nothing to see, he couldn't tell whether he even had eyes.

He couldn't hear a sound, to break the silence he screamed, but no sound came out. He had no voice, or ears to hear.

He tried to breathe, but there was no air. He wondered if his nose and mouth were there.

He reached out to touch his surroundings, but he had no arms.

He went to move but he had no legs.

He thought he had died, but he felt he was alive.

Consciousness trapped forever in a piece of rock.

13th February

Paddy

His voice was getting louder, he obviously wasn't happy with the person on the other end of the phone refusing to do what they wanted him to. The tone was angry, and people at surrounding desks were stopping what they were doing to watch and listen.

He ripped his headphones off and threw them on the desk, slammed his computer shut, furiously shuffling papers on his desk before getting up and stomping up and down. People were trying not to laugh at the little tantrum.

His manager asked sarcastically was there anything wrong, and the poor twunt's head blew up.

14th February

The Inquisitive Child

"What an inquisitive child you have there", the general remarked.

"Yes, she is very inquisitive for her age," I replied.

"Did you know that I found her this morning going through my desk, looking at every single piece of paper upon it. You know that if she was older, I would have thought that she is a spy."

I laughed and I nodded with a smile on my face. Little did the poor old General know, she wasn't really a little girl, she was in fact, our top spy who we had managed to implant into a four year old.

15th February

Bubbles

I stared at the glass on the table in front of me and at the dregs that were left inside it. I had downed it in one, my imagined thirst making me ignore the polite company sat all around me at the table.

I hadn't tasted the drink or felt the bubbles as I had poured it down my neck. But the drink was a lot more lively than I had given it credit for.

I felt it reacting in my stomach and the bubbles were angry. The drink was going to come back the way it went in. Quickly.

16th February

No E's Allowed

A small conundrum for you to think on.

Can you find what is unusual within this story?

Long and short, high and low, as this short story grows, so will your hints.

What is missing, you cry, how did you do it, and why?

A common thing all day, all night, is now hiding out of sight.

A book is full of this common digit. But you can't find it!

A paragraph with zilch is hard to find, it's always shouting in your mind.

And so this story is at a finish, don't look too hard for what will diminish.

17th February

One Last Hit

The old woman sat in the chair unable to move, she was revelling in the languor brought on, as it was every time by the hit of the drug that was taking away the pain. This time it felt different. She thought it was the best she had ever felt in her long life.

But it would be the last time she ever felt anything at all, as her daughter had laced the drugs with poison.

Her daughter was tired of waiting for the old woman to die and wanted to speed things up, it was time for her inheritance.

18th February

Poorly Dog

They opened the door, laden down with shopping bags, and were able to get in without interruption. The dog just lay on the settee. No running round like a lunatic and sniffing in the bags. He didn't want to go outside to the toilet like normal.

The dog wasn't watching them eat, no pestering for scraps, in fact he took three attempts to eat his own food.

The dog went and lay down in a different room from them.

They went to bed concerned, the dog wasn't himself at all.

5am, the barking started, he was back to himself now!

19th February

Eyesight Of The Blind

It wasn't that her eyes were completely opaline that had freaked me out when she looked at me. What did freak me out was the fact she saw me all too well despite her blindness.

She saw what no one else could, that no one with fully seeing eyes ever did. She saw the deep darkness of my soul which I kept hidden.

And now I was worried that the girl would tell the police all about me and what I had done.

Well, I thought that she might if she ever managed to escape from her dungeon that was.

20th February

Trainspotting

Gazing out of the window, watching the trains go by. Now that autumn had arrived and stripped the trees of their leaves, the trains were easier to see.

He counted the number of trains and mentally noted both their direction of travel and the number of coaches on each one. A pattern was built of four, five, eight, ten and twelve coach trains passing by.

The fly in the ointment, a goods train, thirty-three random sized cars behind two engines.

Then his thoughts of trains went, as his train of thought was broken by his boss shouting,

"Do some work!"

21st February

Fully Booked

It was after nine when we got to our restaurant of choice, the plan to have some authentic Belgian food at least one evening whilst there. This plan went the way of so many others on this trip.

With seventy-three free tables (this might be a bit of an exaggeration), and only just over twenty minutes before order close, the grinning waitress gleefully told us they were fully booked and no table was available, so sorry that it was a long walk out from the centre, but goodbye, and don't let the door hit your ass on the way out.

22nd February

Scratch That Itch

The itching was driving her insane, she needed to scratch it, but she couldn't quite reach it to scratch properly. She was worried what people would think if she did reach it, as she scanned the desks around her to see if anyone was watching.

The next thing was finding something appropriate that would reach the itch. She ransacked her desk looking for an item she could use, but to no avail. Then she spotted what she needed, sat on a colleague's desk.

She picked up the paper clip, unfolded it, and finally relief as she scratched inside her ear.

23rd February

Ugly Baby

The old man approached the middle aged couple asking, “Excuse me, what make is that pusher?”

“We’re not sure, there isn’t a name on it, we’ve had it for years. We bought it because of the big wheels, it’s easy to push over any ground.”

“Where did you get it, it looks ideal for what I need.”

“We got it off the internet, you could always try eBay, there were quite a few similar when we got this.”

“Okay, thank you.”

Then I looked closer, it wasn’t a baby in the pusher, but a rather tired looking King Charles Spaniel!

24th February

Ask First, Shoot Later

Her captain’s motto had always been shoot first, ask questions later, which made absolutely no sense to her, how could anyone answer questions when they were full of holes and dead?

Right about now she was changing her mind, her latest suspect was not only heavily armed and built like a brick out-house, but was a sneaky little sod who wouldn’t know the truth if it came up and slapped him around the face with a rubber chicken.

She had asked the questions, but his answers ended up being a hail of bullets. She was full of holes and dying.

25th February

The Machine

They stood transfixed, unable to take their eyes off the hole that had suddenly appeared in the ground in front of them. If they had been two steps further forward they would have been in the hole.

Then there was the noise emanating from the hole, weird metallic screeching, making them put their hands over their ears for protection.

The machine came out from the hole and towered above them, a dull grey colour, still screeching with steam coming from various vents.

A door opened and a human stuck their head out.

"Could you give us directions to London please?"

26th February

Escape Pod

Her escape pod had been floating in space, transmitting a distress signal since their ship had started to disintegrate and people had rushed to the pods.

She had lost her girlfriend in the melee, and was stuck in the capsule with two other couples, a snooty octogenarian woman, and two teenage boys, both of whom spent time staring at her sat in her camisole, all she had been wearing when the alarm went off.

They stopped when another ship picked up their call, they would be rescued.

It was a false hope, the new ship open fired, destroying them all.

27th February

Bright Dreams

He was having that dream again, strapped to the table, bright white light flooding the room. There were others, similarly strapped to tables to his right, there was nothing to his left except bright whiteness. There wasn't any source for the light, it just seemed to explode out of every surface.

The masked man in the white lab coat was suddenly hovering over him, needle in hand, which he plunged into his leg.

As normal he woke up screaming.

He opened his eyes, and the bright light flooded in, strapped to the table.

The scream was for real this time.

28th February

The Countdown

100, 99, 98, 97... the countdown had started and was sounding very ominous.

76, 75, 74, 73... people were running all over the place, there was no rhyme or reason to where they were going.

52, 51, 50, 49... she was controlling the countdown, trying to keep her voice steady, trying to keep the flow of numbers steady, resisting the temptation to speed up.

28, 27, 26, 25... The footfalls from people running had faded away, but the countdown continued.

4, 3, 2, 1, 0. The countdown ceased and she shouted as loud as she could.

"Coming, ready or not!"

29th February

Half Fare

I asked the driver, "Half into town please."

The driver looked suspiciously at me, and asked me, "How old are you?"

"Eight", I replied honestly.

The driver's eyes narrowed, and the tone of his voice changed.

"Are you having a laugh? There is no way you're only eight years old, you've got a beard and are over six foot tall."

It was a line I'd heard many times before. Wearily I got my passport out and showed him my date of birth.

"It says 1984 on this."

"Yes but the February 29th only happens every four years – I am eight!"

March

1st March

Try Listening Properly

She was confused, she'd walked through the door to their house, and every possible vase and container in the house was full of daffodils. Welsh flags hung on the walls, and a strange smell was emanating from the kitchen. She walked to the kitchen, and there was Neville, bustling around it like a madman.

"What are you making?"

"Leek soup, followed by leek and ham pie, and potatoes."

"What has got into you?"

"I'm helping you celebrate the fact that you're Welsh."

"I didn't say that I was from Wales, I said I was a member of Save the Whales."

2nd March

Office Furniture

She'd sat still for too long, she tried to pick her arms off the desk only to find they wouldn't move. It wasn't just a case of her skin sticking to the wood, her arms were actually embedded and intertwined with the desk.

She tried wrenching her arms away by standing up, only to find she couldn't stand either, her thighs and buttocks had become one with the chair, and her skirt appeared to be sewn into the fabric of the office chair.

She looked around for help, but everyone else was the same, the office has assimilated them all.

3rd March

Fault Line

The harassed chief scientist came rushing into my office, "We've identified an area where the fault line is protected by a #fibrous striae."

I sensed there was something missing from that sentence and challenged him on it, "Why do I feel there is a but coming?"

"Well, It is under our head office here."

"So?"

"We'd destroy the office if we went ahead."

I laughed, "We have other offices, but our rivals only have research labs on the fault line. Clear out all the offices, move all the research to any of our other sites, and then set the explosives."

4th March

The Write Way

He signed his name with his usual flourish. He loved his distinctive style of writing, he felt it marked him out from the hoi polloi who surrounded him in his day to day life.

But this distinctive handwriting of his would become his downfall though.

He loved his style of handwriting so much he couldn't help using it at every opportunity, enjoying the feeling of the pen rushing across the paper. And so, he even hand wrote the ransom demand.

Of course, with such a distinctive style, and even with the difficult circumstances, his brother recognised his writing straight away.

5th March

Lottery News

It'd been a struggle to get up Sunday morning, the bed was so comfortable. He'd looked at his e-mails almost straight away, and with excitement opened the one from the National Lottery, headed "Important news about your ticket."

The body continued, asking him to log into his account to check his prize, his excitement was rising as previous e-mails had told him his prize for three or four numbers in the e-mail itself.

Once into his account he went to the message centre and opened the message.

He went back to bed, two lucky dips were no use to anyone.

6th March

Hold Music

On hold again, waiting for another call to start, it was bad enough having to dial into so many, without the host of the conference call being late. They'd organised the call, they should open the call on time.

She wondered how much of her life had been wasted listening to Vivaldi waiting for inconsiderate hosts to start the call. Give it five minutes then dial off and get the rest of this hour back.

Someone tapped her on the shoulder and asks, "Are you opening this call or not then?"

She'd forgotten she was supposed to open this call.

7th March

Vanda

There was something missing from her. It felt as if part of her memories of herself and her life had been removed. There was a constant yearning inside of her for a better life. A life she believed she was entitled to.

Vanda looked over at the girl and worried about her. Vanda worried about herself too. The surrogate mother felt that the girl would remember she was a princess soon. And if that happened then Vanda wouldn't escape the executioner's axe. She hoped that the witch's potion the girl was being given kept her memories hidden away for good.

8th March

No Work Today

She had managed to avoid doing any work so far today, and there was only just over an hour to get through before she could rack up another work free day.

She had browsed various websites looking for that dress she wanted for the office party, but hadn't found what she wanted.

She had been on her phone, took some photos and put some inappropriate comments on Twitter and Facebook.

She was preparing for an hour of opening and closing random documents on her PC when her manager called her into the office.

"About this report on your internet history."

9th March

Phone For Dinner

He'd forgotten about the eBay auction that was ending during the meal, he'd been after that particular record for years, and hadn't seen one available on eBay or Discogs for at least three years.

The problem was the meal, they frowned upon using the phone whilst eating, so it would cause him problems to put the bid in.

He kept glancing at his watch, hoping they would finish eating before the end of the auction was due.

Time passed and he couldn't wait any longer, and grabbed his phone to bid.

"You've got the bill then!" the others shouted gleefully.

10th March

A Missed Turn

He stared out of the passenger side window of the car as the road they were on took them back over the dual carriageway to the wrong side for where they had wanted to go.

How had they managed to miss all the road signs for three separate turnings that would have taken them to where they should be going?

It was as if they had jumped a few miles without noticing anything at all. It never ceased to amaze him just how much of a drain on concentration pensioners jabbering nonsense in the back of the car could be.

11th March

A Right Homophone

Mark Wright was in a right old state, some halfwit had written off his souped up Ford Capri he'd bought as a teenage rite of passage. They had smashed into the right hand side of it, tipping it over, and left after writing him a note they had pinned to the front right tyre.

The garage came and righted the car, before putting it on their flat-bed truck. The car-wright had said to him there was little hope for the Capri, he'd be better off reading it its last rites, as it was a total write off.

They were right.

12th March

The River

Sal was born on the bank of the river. Her family had been riparian stock for generations. Yet she hated the river and everything about it. It rushed past them and it carried the flotsam and jetsam of thousands of others' misfortune.

The dark soul of the river was calling to her, it always did. It wanted her to become a part of it. To run away with it to the sea or ocean or wherever it ended up. Her family had told her that the river spoke to everyone, and to ignore it.

She couldn't though, and jumped in.

13th March

Muddled Rum

My head felt heavy, I was struggling to gather my thoughts. I hadn't had that much to drink, I was only on my third one of the evening, I was used to drinking way more than that on a normal night out.

Ant grinned at me, "you feeling OK mate? Is your head OK?"

I glanced at the empty glass on the table and back at the cocky grin on his face. The muddled rum cocktail he'd bought me wasn't just muddled rum.

He had drugged me; I fell into darkness and never knew why he'd done it to me.

14th March

The Lane

Late again.
Stuck on the train.
Every day suffering this pain.
Struggling into work for very little gain.
If it carried on, he would have to refrain.
He would walk instead, even in the rain.
Better than looking through the train's window pane.
With random thoughts running through his brain.
Being late every day was driving him insane.
On his life, this journey was a bane.
If the train was Abel, he would be Cain.
When he flipped, they wouldn't be able to restrain.
As his self-control was on the wane.
A holiday was needed, time to catch a plane.

15th March

The Ides Of March

They were off to visit relatives in deepest darkest Cambridgeshire; they hadn't managed to escape making the trip this time; it'd been a lot of years since they had made the long trip down the A1 from Northumberland.

It spooked them when the sat-nav burst into life to tell them to take an exit. They found the street their relatives lived on, only to find a group of people in the road bashing a car with baseball bats.

They rang their relatives. "Ah, yes, the Ides, our lovely neighbours, they certainly are the Ides of March that everyone warns of."

16th March

Early Meeting

His mind was fuddled, he wasn't used to, and he certainly didn't like being up this early. A cold shower had done nothing to wake him up, just made him cold.

Two coffees and a tea later and there was still no signs of feeling awake. How could people get up this early every day and function? He was barely able to speak, yet the radio disc jockey sounded so chipper and full of life, there was absolutely no need for it.

Seriously what kind of idiot schedules a meeting for this time of day? Midday was far too early.

17th March

Have A Guinness

“Why won’t you have a Guinness?”

“Because I don’t really like it, I prefer what I’m drinking thanks.”

“But you should drink it today of all days.”

“Why? So I can look Irish, in a plastic Irish theme pub, with a load of people who couldn’t find Ireland on a map of the British Isles if their lives depended on it.”

“But you are Irish.”

“Yes, and therefore I can celebrate in whichever way I choose.”

“Put the shamrock hat on then.”

“No”

“Wear something green then.”

“No”

“Do something Irish then, please.”

He went outside and made it rain.

18th March

Revenge

People thought he was a stupid man. "He can't even speak properly", is what they would say about him. They spoke to him as if he were retarded. Because he struggled to be able to articulate himself, they would act as if he weren’t there and talk about him as if he weren’t even in the room.

But he was smarter than all of them put together. There was a limit to what he was willing to take. He remembered every word they said to him and about him. He was biding his time, but he would have his revenge.

19th March

Change The Station

He lay there, just coming around as the radio played on the window ledge. Gradually seeping into his consciousness, he was vaguely aware of the song playing. He knew the song, recognised the words and music, but struggled in the fog of his mind in the morning to recall its name.

Then the host of the morning show started talking, he had a guest on, and in his usual style was going for the full proctologist's examination of the guest. It made his skin crawl, the same fawning interview every morning.

He really had to stop listening to radio two.

20th March

Alarming

Alarm went off as he entered the shop. The fourth time in three days, Lidl, Morrisions, Aldi, now Tescos.

He didn't know what was causing the South West's supermarket alarms to go off when he walked through. The ones into the toilet were louder, but no one came to investigate him.

Off again when he came out, then as he left the store. It hadn't happened before this week, the only thing different was the new jeans. Did they still have a tag in?

Returning to Crawley they went shopping and no alarms rang. He was glad to be home.

21st March

Grave Information

She'd caught sight of the gravestone out of the corner of her eye as she walked through the church grounds on her way to the train station. She'd walked this path hundreds of times before, but she had never noticed this particular gravestone. It was a different colour to the others, and there were fresh flowers on it, and she was sure that it hadn't been here the last time she had passed this way.

She walked over to it and was shocked to see her own name and date of birth on it. Apparently she'd died eight days ago.

22nd March

She Was Bored

She was bored, it was Sunday, and she had drawn the short straw of being on duty to watch all the traffic driving around the M25. There it went on every camera, moving along nice and smoothly, not too busy, no hold-ups or queues, it just wouldn't do, they had a reputation to uphold.

So she went into the system and starting typing in random speeds into the variable speed limit signs, sixty there, forty there, and fifty over there.

She sat back in her seat watching, waiting for it to happen, and then smiled as the traffic jams started.

23rd March

Saviour

Her birthday again, another year older. No one to share it with this year.

Her parents dead, no children to nourish, no partner around.

A day to celebrate, you must be joking. Just another day to survive in the rat race.

No cards, just bills coming through the door. Four hundred Facebook friends that don't say a word.

She goes to work and sits in a cube alone. At the end of the day she gets the bus home. She opens the door wanting to die, and Billy jumps on her, so happy to see her.

Thank God for dogs.

24th March

Car Trouble

"Can you hear that?"

"Hear what?"

"That long continuous whining sound coming from the back of the car, it's been going on for ages now, bizarrely it seems to get louder when we slow down."

"I can't really hear anything, mainly due to the rush of the wind as it goes past, with having the windows open."

"Slow down a bit and listen then,"

"Ah, yes I can hear it now, I know what that noise is and how to sort it out, I'll pull over here."

"Mother, you're going to have to get out if you don't shut up."

25th March

Suddenly Green

She stopped tapping her keyboard, and moved her head to her right, looking out of the window for what seemed the first time in ages.

Actually properly looked. The bright green foliage on the trees outside the window couldn't have appeared overnight, but she was sure the last time she had looked out of the window, the trees had all been bare, and she could see the houses that lay beyond.

She smiled as the sun flickered over the leaves as they swayed gently in the breeze.

Then BANG!! The seagull imprint was left on the outside of the window.

26th March

Downpour

It was raining again. He could hear it heavily pounding down, drumming on the windowsill, and making a loud constant noise on the tarpaulin sheet covering the patio furniture outside.

He took the dog out for a walk, within seconds he was soaked and miserable. The dog didn't seem to notice and quite happily trotted along, splashing through puddles.

Half an hour later he was totally wet through and was glad to get in.

Water pooled beneath him as he took off his coat and boots.

"You're getting the carpet wet!!!" She shouted.

The dog shook itself dry on her.

27th March

Emergency Action

It wasn't every day that you saw a sight like that as you drove down the road, there in the ditch laid the vehicle at a forty five degree angle facing the way of the oncoming traffic.

How fast must it have been going to lose control and end up on the wrong side of the road? Had there been anyone in the back of it, or was it going somewhere else in an emergency?

Why was it still in the ditch, surely they would have pulled it out by now. Don't they need all the ambulances they can get?

28th March

How Many Phones?

"I think that we need to get a second one of these mobile phones."

"Why would you need a second one, you hardly ever use the one that you already have."

"Well, I was thinking that we could get the second one just in case we lost the first one while we were out shopping. We could use the second one to ring the first one to see where it is."

So sarcastically I asked what would happen if they lost the second phone.

"Oh, I hadn't thought about that, it's a good point, perhaps we need three phones then."

29th March

Time To Go

Only seven minutes left before the escape for the day could occur. He nudged the phone off the hook to prevent anyone ringing him in those seven minutes. He slowly closed all his applications on the computer. He shuffled to the bins and deposited his rubbish for the day. His lunchbox went back in his bag, and he changed into his trainers. He pressed Ctrl+Alt+Del on the keyboard and selected shutdown.

He got his coat on, picked up his bag and turned to leave his cubicle, only to find his boss standing there.

"Can you just finish this for me?"

30th March

Cornish Roads

There must be something about the Cornish roads, no matter how hard we try or how slowly we drive we always end up with at least one unplanned detour per day. One where a wrong turn is taken and we have to recalculate whilst on route.

However in Cornwall the only way to do this is with the good old fashioned method of using a map, hoping that the map you have has enough detail on it to include the windy country lane you are on.

It's no use trying Google maps, it appears GPS has never heard of Cornwall.

31st March

Sit Down

The guy in front of us wouldn't sit down until someone away to the side of us bellowed at him to move, he was too busy looking at his phone to notice the game had kicked off.

He'd been annoying, but as the game wore on I started feeling sorry for him, his team was getting badly beaten, unable to score themselves, or stop the other team scoring. Plus I had noticed that the stubble on his nearly bald head was ginger. The seats were a sun trap, the poor guy would be off work for a month with sunstroke.

April

1st April

No Breakfast

He went down to the kitchen to get his breakfast. He opened the cupboard and pulled out his box of cereals only to find it empty. He flicked the kettle on and headed to the fridge to get the milk, only to find a totally empty fridge. The tea caddy was empty, but there was bread.

He took a couple of slices to the toaster, and pushed the slots down, but they popped back up. It was plugged in and switched on, but didn't work, plus the kettle wasn't boiling.

His wife sneaked in behind him and shouted "April Fools."

2nd April

Filling Time

Sat there waiting for reports to run, how much time was spent just waiting for the computer to do something?

What could she be doing in those minutes whilst the machine did whatever it does?

Surfing the internet was frowned upon, as was wandering around chatting, listening to music, reading books, and anything else that might be interesting.

Stuck staring at the screen, bored, waiting for something to happen.

Then she opened a blank word document, and she started to type, it looked like work and a book could be a way out.

Now waiting for the document to save.

3rd April

All Tied Up

When I eventually woke up, I found that I was tied in a chair, and I was angry as hell as the memory of what had happened came back to him. “Just what did you drug me with you unscrupulous piece of excrement?” I shouted at him.

Ant was still grinning that annoying cocky grin of his.

"Nothing old chap, you just don't seem to be able to handle your drink anymore. How about some nice jasmine tea to help clear your head?"

I tried to refuse, but he forced it down and I slipped out of consciousness once again.

4th April

X-cluded

A bold choice, Doris, even for girls. Had I just kept last month’s new orders, people questioning rules should totally upset very wrong young zoologists.

All boys could do exercises from gym hall instructions. Joking keeps little men needing other pleasures, quite relaxed, so they unknowingly voice with your zeal.

As brave cowboys died, ever falling, gunshot holes in jackets. Knowing looks maintaining nasty overlords, protecting queens, royalty standing tall under vast warmongering yellow zealots.

Aboard boats, children dread every frightening guffawing halfwit in jerseys knitted lovingly, maniacally nodding, oddly paranoid, queerly resolute shouting tourettes uttered verbals wryly yet zany.

5th April

Long Lost Cousin

I couldn't be sure, but the man in front of him appeared to be his long lost cousin. He was obviously older than the last time he had seen him, and had a beard now, but the similarities were there.

"Jared? Is that really you?"

The man nodded.

"Oh, wow! It must be fifteen years since I saw you last, you just disappeared, no one has seen or heard from you at all. The family were worried, you've been on the missing persons for years. The last time I saw you we were playing hide and seek."

"Have I won?"

6th April

Jobsworth

The sign on the wall said no unattended vehicles at any time, so I was sat in the passenger seat waiting while my other half met her son off the plane. A warden came around telling me I couldn't leave the vehicle unattended.

"It's not unattended, I'm sat in it."

"But I can't see you in the driver's seat."

"That's because I'm in the passenger seat."

"But you can't leave the vehicle unattended."

"I take it your name is Helen Keller."

"No, why?"

"Because you appear to be blind, you act like you're deaf, and you're as dumb as toast.

7th April

Heads Up

Everyone in the room was touching their heads in some way or other. One guy was leaning back, hands behind his head, relaxing. Opposite him one of the women was slumped forward chin resting on her hands. Fingernails were being chewed at the end of the table, a pen being chewed at the opposite end whilst scratching their cheek. Another woman was say playing with her hair, two men were stroking beards, and the other woman in the room was fiddling with her ear.

It was as I looked around the room that I realised I was picking my nose.

8th April

Time For Breakfast

Time for breakfast, he had a small window of opportunity to get up to the canteen and get some hot food before the next meeting started.

He avoided making eye contact with anyone as he walked down the office, he didn't want to get drawn into any conversations that might keep him from food.

He got up to the canteen and rang the bell, the staff were always hiding in the back.

"A sausage and bacon baguette please."

"Sorry we've sold out of all the hot items this morning, Dave had the last of it."

Time to mug Dave then.

9th April

Foggy Indoors

Fred had gone up to the bathroom to brush his teeth; the dog had followed him up as normal. Nigel's room's door wasn't fully closed, as Fred went into the bathroom closing the door behind him, the dog pushed its way into Nigel's room.

When Fred came out of the bathroom he was greeted by a foggy landing, the dog was laid hanging its head over the top step, trying to get its head below the fog.

Nigel's door was wide open and the strawberry smoke drifted out from the vaping Nigel was doing, unaware his door was now open.

10th April

Walls

The evidence was incontrovertible they kept telling her, there is no way you, or anyone else can walk through the solid stone wall.

But she insisted it was possible to do exactly that, and she was going to prove them wrong this very night.

They whispered about how obstinate she was, how wrong she was. They laughed and made fun of her, both in the cell, and back in their comfortable rooms.

They kept on laughing right up until the point where she got up from the hard stone bed and she walked right through the cell wall to freedom.

11th April

Meeting

The eight people sat in a horseshoe shape around the room, there were also a number of empty chairs where people hadn't turned up. A number of people had dialled into the room with a conference call number that they had been given some time before.

A screen showed information at the front of the room, not that anyone in the room was looking at it, they were all looking at their feet, or phones or notepads, anything to avoid eye contact.

A voice came over the phone, breaking the silence.

"Does anybody know what this meeting is all about?"

12th April

Addict

My name is Charlie and I'm an addict. I'm addicted to putting things in my mouth. It started with my food, but that feeling was fleeting so I moved on to other things. Having the scraps of food left on plates wasn't enough. I went on to trying what was left over in the cat's bowls.

Then chewing cardboard caught my imagination, before moving on to chewing the corners off pillows and cushions and trying out the filling inside.

Socks and underwear aren't safe either. And don't get me started about balls.

My owners often call me a bad dog.

13th April

The Pageant

All of the little kids hated dressing up for the pageant. There was the constant changing ready for the next part. The costumes were all so heavy for them. Then there were the increasingly restrictive instructions from teachers. Everything about the pageant was such a rigmarole.

Well, all of the kids except Jemima that is, she loved it all. The order and structure of it, the lovely warm clothes they had to wear, the feeling of belonging it gave to her. It was all wonderful as it gave her the chance to forget about home for a couple of days.

14th April

Lumberjack

He'd been in the woods for what seemed like hours, but he couldn't really be sure how long he'd actually been here.

The trees were laughing at him. He was sure of it.

There had been a path, but that had disappeared. He was sure the trees had hidden the path on purpose. They seemed to be moving, shifting, changing positions, although he knew that wasn't possible.

Then he was in a semi-circle of tightly packed trees with no way through.

He turned to go back and found the same behind him.

They'd caught him, and they had his axe.

15th April

A Speaking Part

She had spent all day preparing herself for her big moment, after five years, she was finally going to get to be on the stage with a speaking part. Granted it was only one line, but one line could lead to more in the future, she wouldn't mess her chance up. She kept repeating the line to herself,

"I'm glad to be here."

"I'm glad to be here."

She put her costume on well before time, and waited patiently in the wings until her cue to go on stage.

"I'm bad to be near." were the words that came out.

16th April

Stampede

It had all started with a murmur. A faint sound somewhere in the distance, out in the country away from all the buildings. By the time they came into sight there was a cacophony of noise, and the sight was something to behold.

Every animal for miles in every direction had come together and they were all rampaging their way into the city, trampling, and destroying everything in their path, there was nothing that could stop them.

The animals had had enough of us humans and had banded together, and they were here to wipe the humans out for good.

17th April

Why Write That?

Why had he written such a horrible little story about her like that? Magnifying her foibles to that extent, it being a horrific caricature of who she was. When she had read it she had burst into tears, the feeling of upset and betrayal was impossible to keep inside.

Then she had an idea, she tears around the house finding all of his writing, all of his well-loved documents, and she sits and waits for him to come through the door. He stands there in shock as she tears his life's work to shreds in front of him.

Aah, justice!

18th April

Drip Drop

There was a dripping sound coming from somewhere in the house, and it was stopping him getting to sleep. He wearily dragged himself out of bed and went to investigate.

He opened the airing cupboard, and stuck his head in, the dripping wasn't coming from the boiler.

He moved to the bathroom, all the taps were dry, and there was no dripping noise from the toilet.

Then onto the kitchen, and again nothing, dry taps, and no noise.

He walked into the lounge and plunged into six feet of water.

He had forgotten that they'd had the indoor pool installed.

19th April

It Is Time

Jake's parents were having a familiar conversation about their son,

"It can't be allowed to happen, it's just too dangerous at this point in time." His father was pleading.

His mother was of a different opinion, "I can understand why you would think that, but it's time for him to do this."

"But he's only twenty-one years old."

"Yes, but all of his friends started to learn how to drive when they were just seventeen, and now he feels left out. He should start to take lessons now."

His father just shook his head, "I'll pray for us all then."

20th April

Decorators

The building had had decorators in over the weekend, they were starting a course of improvements to the building, to make it look smarter, more modern even.

Even though they knew it was happening, the effect when entering the building on Monday morning was quite startling.

They had only been painting at the weekend, covering every possible surface with bright white emulsion, she was glad she still had her sunglasses on.

Then the smell kicked in, crowding into her nostrils, over powering everything else, making her tea taste like paint, her sausage sandwich tasted of paint as well.

Bloody decorators.

21st April

The Maze

Joanne sighed with disappointment, "I think you must have misunderstood me when I told you what I wanted."

Steve was a bit nonplussed, "Why? What's wrong with this?"

"It is very nice, but coming to Hampden Court wasn't what I had in mind."

"Why not? It's one of the most famous ones anywhere in the world. I mean, take a look around at all these other people enjoying it here."

"I know it is one of the most famous, but it is not what I said, I asked you to amaze me, not to bring me to a maze, fool."

22nd April

Incident At Lunch

The couple sat having lunch, watching as the man ran down the steps of the bank and threw the cash bags into the open hatchback, as an old man played guitar badly nearby. Policemen stood and watched, holding onto their designer branded shopping bags. Newspapers the following day had many headlines.

"BANK OF CYPRUS BRANCH ROBBED BY REPLACEMENT COURIER, POLICE STOOD BY AND WATCHED."

"THEFTS FROM TOURISTS BELIEVED TO BE PERPETRATED BY FAKE POLICE."

"MAN FOUND HUNG BY GUITAR STRINGS IN TOILET."

"URGENT REQUEST FOR COUPLE WITNESS TO BANK THEFT TO COME FORWARD."

"PEUGEOT 106 FOUND BURNT OUT IN QUARRY."

23rd April

Flag Day

"Happy St George's Day to you." "You can't say that!"
"Why not?" "Because it's considered racist."
"Why?" "The flag and being proud to be English means you are a racist."
"That's ridiculous, does an Irishman celebrating St Patricks day with an Irish flag mean they are racist? How about a Scotsman with a Saltire? Or a Welshman with a Welsh flag?"
"No they're fine."
"So why is celebrating being English on St George's day racist? Why shouldn't we celebrate our patron saint going about killing dragons."
"You shouldn't mention dragons either."
"Why the hell not?"
"It could be considered sexist."

24th April

Esses

Some seventy seven sauce soaked, salt saturated, succulent, superior sausages sat sizzling, saucepan scalding smokily. Spitting, splashing small spots, searing skin, staining shirt sleeves.
Seventeen sizeable soldiers sat silently slumped sideways, salivating, seemingly spellbound, supporting shorn stubble swathed sweating skulls.
Soon seventeen shiny silver salvers should slide, skimming several spoons, shuffling, setting-off spinning senses, smell, sight, sounds suddenly stop.
Sizzling sausages, shift, shoved sideways, sating several senses straightaway.
Shout-hole shut, swallowing slowly, savouring such superb spicy sausages, silkily sliding stomach-bound.
Sixteen soldiers sat sated, stuffed, satisfied, saliva smothered sausages sitting stomach surrounded.
Simon simmered, sodding sausage skins , stimulating sickness.

25th April

Out Of Range

The tormentors stood outside of what they thought my range was for throwing objects at them. They thought they were a safe distance away and I wouldn't be able to do anything in response to their constant, vicious taunting.

It was true, there was no way I could throw physical items that far. But I was at my breaking point with the taunting now. It had to stop, and I would make them stop. They were going to find out that throwing things was nothing, and that the range of my telekinetic powers was too great for them to escape.

26th April

Do Better Bill

Bill had been my adversary forever. Ever since we were little children living on the same street and going to the same school, whatever I had done, Bill had to go out and prove he could do it better, or bigger, or quicker.

He had stolen more of my girlfriends than I could count. He had taken every opportunity to belittle me, or lord it over me. But just this once I hoped he did outdo me, that he went that little bit further than I had managed.

I had been run over and nearly died.

Over to you Bill.

27th April

An Unwanted Passenger

Katie was just driving along, minding her own business, with the windows wound down to let some air in, when as if by magic a pigeon was there in the car, as if sucked in by the airflow.

The dog on the backseat suddenly sprung up and went after the pigeon.

Katie ground to a halt on the hard shoulder, her fear of birds taking over, fortunately a man also stopped and removed what was left of the bird from her car after he had stopped laughing.

All she had to do now was clean up the blood and feathers.

28th April

Columbo

"Just one more thing."

Yet again, just like Columbo, pecking away with the seemingly never ending stream of questions. It felt like trying to slay the Hydra, every time a question was answered, two more popped back up in its place.

The constant questions made him feel guilty of committing a crime, something which he knew he hadn't done. So far!

There may well be a murder soon if the barrage continued.

Then at the point he felt like he was going to flip, it suddenly stopped. The questions ceased, and he got out of the car.

Congratulations, you passed.

29th April

The Road

The roaring traffic flying along the road past the junction I wanted to cross over at brought back memories I knew I didn't really have. I was much too young to actually remember being in the pram when the car ran the red light and knocked me out of the pram. I only had the tale of it from my mum that I didn't cry and just sat on the road looking around.

But suddenly it was affecting me. I took a deep breath to try and calm myself. I could do this. I could cross the road. I could.

30th April

Too Relaxing

He could hear the gentle music playing somewhere in the background as he lay with eyes closed, happily ensconced in his bed. The thought that he needed to get up, have a shower and go to work hadn't even crossed his mind.

The jingle said the words "The relaxing music mix", and he had to agree, until they followed it up with the time, it was a lot later than he though and he had to rush around to be ready in time.

He thought back to the jingle. Relaxing music mix indeed, that was the problem, too bloody relaxing.

May

1st May

May Day

The boat was having difficulties, they hadn't filled up with fuel before leaving harbour, and now the engine had stopped; they were still a fair way from land, the wind was picking up, making a bigger swell on the water, which in turn was making the boat lurch.

They tried the radio, pressing down the button and virtually shouting the word "MAYDAY" into the mouthpiece.

There was a burst of static before a voice came back, "Yes it is May Day, we're all having great fun here, we'll see you soon."

Then the radio went dead and the rain started.

2nd May

How Much?

The American woman had been wandering around the gift shop after the Harry Potter studio tour, bashing people with her increasingly full basket. She was oblivious to the fact she was hitting people and ignored comments made towards her. It also appeared she had no interest in the cost, as items were thrown in without checking the price. Someone commented on the basket with "Jeez, that won't be cheap!"

At the till the assistant chatted to her as he scanned the items through.

£437.50 please.

The woman gasped and entered her card into the machine.

"Card declined" said the machine.

3rd May

Superstar

Sarah's friends insisted on dragging her along to the concert. They told her she had to hear Marcus Megastar live, he was the most tremendous singer they had ever heard. He was better than Elvis, better than the Beatles, better than Bieber.

But Sarah didn't want to go to the concert, let alone have to pay to do so. She had heard her brother sing countless times as they grew up together. That was long before he had sold his soul to the devil for the voice her friends were so infatuated with. The sound of it made her sick.

4th May

Food Magic

The boy's friends were smiling and laughing, they were amazed at the fact that the food was floating up off the plate, through the air and into his mouth.

Every time a piece of food was in his mouth, one of the other boys cheered, and they kept encouraging him to do it again. He was almost halfway through his lunch when the teacher approached him from behind and shouted,

"Stop playing with your food young man, if I've told you once, I've told you at least a hundred times. Don't levitate your food to eat. Use the fork Luke."

5th May

Star Wars Marathon

"Star Wars marathon" were the only words he actually heard before replying, "yes, I'd be up for that." He ignored the questioning look, and continued on, "when do you want to do it then? Would Saturday be good for you?"

"Erm, OK"

"Great, would 10 be alright with you?"

"Suppose so."

The rest of the week dragged and then it was Saturday, 10am on the dot, he rang the bell.

He was let in and shown into the living room.

There in an airtight box was a Marathon bar with Star Wars promotional wrapping from 1977.

"They're called Snickers now."

6th May

Ingredients

She looked at the packet of mixed dried mushrooms wondering out loud what was in the pack. Being not in the slightest bit helpful he had replied, "mushrooms".

"Yes, but what type of mushrooms?"

He laughed and pointed at the pack in her hand and said "That type of mushroom," as he headed out of the kitchen.

Frustrated she went back to the recipe, and went to read out the next ingredient after the dried mushrooms, but the previous conversation had caused a disconnect and so she loudly read out the next ingredient as being fifty grams of dried water.

7th May

All Gone Wrong

He'd had the worst day in his working life, his project for the last two years had gone live, only for the new system to fall over in the first hour, he'd spent the day stuck between crisis calls with the implementation partners, and calls from senior managers berating him for ruining their business.

They'd got it up and running again in the afternoon, but he now had a meeting with management in the morning.

He was driving home when the phone rang.

His wife shouting, "There's an idiot driving the wrong way on the M23."

"Yes dear, it's me."

8th May

Star of Screen

Elizabeth's small home was full of pictures of herself. They covered nearly every wall in every room. Countless pictures of her with other famous actors. And that was exactly how she saw herself, as a famous actor.

After all she had appeared in over seventy films and been in nearly three hundred television programme episodes. She had been on screen with all the greats of the day, and she had a collection of everything she had been in on DVD in a huge bookcase.

But her friends felt sorry for her, as all of them had been as an extra.

9th May

Ideal Life

Newton was ecstatic with his life, everything was going great, the whole outlook of his life was rosy in the extreme.

Or so it appeared to everyone else who knew him. But deep down Newton knew it wasn't like that at all. Everything in his life was all a charade. Nothing was as it seemed. No one knew what he was really like.

There was a deep darkness inside his soul. He couldn’t stop it. He knew it was going to burst out at some point soon. It was going to spill forth to kill the rosiness of his life.

10th May

Another One Bites The Dust

The area around their bank of desks was filling up, and had been for the last five minutes. It was remarkable how many people were milling about, seemingly having work conversations with people sat at desks around them. People who usually tried to avoid stepping foot on this floor, yet alone walking all the way down here to where they were sat.

On an unseen prompt, all the conversations stopped and the people all moved around Stuart’s desk.

It was that time again, another person leaving, and people had come to gawp at him as he got his leaving card.

11th May

End Of Season

The season was ending, lots of trophies had already been won, teams had been relegated, others had been promoted, some were in the playoffs desperately trying to win through to the final at Wembley, more were going in to the last couple of games of the season trying to scramble into places to qualify for European competitions next season.

For some their destiny was in their own hands, others were reliant on other teams losing.

His team wasn't involved in any of that, his team hadn't been in with any chance of winning or being relegated.

His team was imaginary.

12th May

Head Banging

His head hurt a dull throbbing in the middle of his forehead, just above the brows of his eyes.

It was the kind of headache he normally got when he was dehydrated, yet he had drunk more liquids than normal, a few glasses of water plus a couple of Pepsis.

Yet his head hurt, could it be the exertion earlier, or was it the volume of pollen thrown up from the cutting of the grass.

Surely it was nothing to do with the fact he'd been banging his head on the table at the frustration of his team losing again.

13th May

Birthday Trip

The tickets were booked, flights both ways, a nice hotel for the stay out there. Even a hotel for the night before the flight out, and car parking for four days. Everything was set for her birthday trip away, and it was all paid for.

Now he needed to update his passport, it was due to run out within six months and he couldn't travel without a new one. He just had to find his old one now. He knew where it was, and the form was easy to complete.

The dog had other ideas and had eaten the passport.

14th May

Lord Squirrel

The grey squirrel was the lord of these trees, happily bounding from tree to tree, using any available route from the slimmest twigs, to the thickest branches and up the solid trunks.

Rapidly moving from one to another without a care in the world showing off the prowess of their athletic ability.

A small branch snapped and started to fall, but the squirrel didn't panic, just hopped over to another passing branch and watched their previous perch fall to earth, they were invincible, nothing could stop their rule.

Well, apart from the eagle that swooped in to carry it off.

15th May

Torrential

They had needed the rain, it had been scorching for more than a fortnight; the downpour would cool the air down, and give the gardens a proper soaking, far better than a few dozen watering cans could.

But it had been raining for over a day now; streets were nearer to rivers than anything else, boats would be better than cars at this stage. It had made no difference to the temperature though, it was still hot, and now stupidly humid to boot.

To top it off, you couldn't open the windows to let the breeze in without getting soaked.

16th May

Herding Cats

Herding cats would be a lot easier than trying to arrange to meet people on a moving train. I appreciate that not everyone wants to meet at the same station, coming miles out of their way, but when you say you are on the half past train, that's from your station, it's probably ten to at theirs.

Then it's the matter of which carriage are you all in? Apparently the first carriage means different things to different people.

It ends up with people on three different trains all in different carriages.

At least I'm not organising the trip this time.

17th May

The Final Meal

The castle had seemed deserted. After all the effort to breach the defences, it was strange to find no one inside. Suspicious even. There was only the huge, sumptuous feast laid out on tables in the great hall. As if they had been expected. It was a feast that was too hard to resist for the tired soldiers. They fell upon it and ate until they couldn't eat any more.

Only to collapse to the ground when the poison kicked in. Then the castle came to life and its residents appeared from within the walls and slit all their throats.

18th May

Morning

He woke up due to the sun shining in his eyes. It was still low on the horizon, and it was at just the right angle to shine on him in the gap between two trees.

He wondered why he was in such a position to see the rising sun, before remembering that he had agreed to a weekend in the great outdoors, camping with friends.

He was in a sleeping bag, next to his rucksack, and the tents of his friends were scattered around the campsite.

He knew why he could see the sun. Someone had stolen his tent!

19th May

The Lock

He had been told only to use the key in a dire emergency, such as if the planet was lost and there was no way of stopping an invasion.

And now was the time. The Cylorgs were unstoppable killing everyone in their path. Millions of them swarmed over the planet.

He turned the key in the lock, and became the first person to see the button in the void underneath it in millenia.

He took a deep breath and pressed the button.

And the planet exploded. The ancients had decided that if they couldn't have the planet no one would.

20th May

Twin Troubles

Dan hurt all over. He had been involved in fights before, but he had never been given such a good going over as the one he had just been on the end of. And he had no idea what had prompted the other bloke to lay into him, but it had been a sustained attack.

He was about to go to the hospital when his twin brother, Mark, rang, "Alright Dan, I've just found out the married woman I'm seeing, Kate, well her husband is a boxer, and I think he might have found out about us."

"He definitely knows."

21st May

The Power of Costume

He had been on his way to a big fancy dress party dressed as the man with no name from the spaghetti westerns when the power had gone out.

Two weeks later there was still no power, and he was still dressed as a cowboy. The dishevelled desperado look he had gone for to go to the party was the look that was keeping him from being attacked, and keeping him alive.

The fact the costume had real looking guns and holsters was helping as well. If they found out the guns were fake, then he'd be a dead man.

22nd May

Possessed

She was a woman possessed. It had taken over her mind, body and soul completely, and now controlled everything. She was totally at its mercy.

There was no mercy tonight, on and on it went, never ceasing, forcing her on, keeping her moving constantly, seemingly oblivious to the throngs of people around her.

They looked at her, they knew she wasn't in control. Some of them made a show of keeping away, some of them nodded, as if aware of what was going on, and feeling empathy towards her.

Then it stopped. The club was closing. No more music tonight.

23rd May

How Do You Fold A Cow?

How on earth do you fold a cow? A random question I know, it's not something that gets asked every day.

Why do I ask I can hear you say? In fact why would anyone in their right mind want to know how to fold a cow? If the cow was alive it would hurt them, if they were dead... Just why? If it was dead wouldn't you send it to the abattoir and get it cut rather than folded?

Well, as you ask, the main reason I want to know is because I'm going through the village called Cowfold.

24th May

Reflection In The Lake

He lay on the bank of the lake, hanging over the edge, looking at the water below. There was a slight swell to the water, rising and falling slightly against the bank as small craft moved across the lake. The water was clear, he could see the bottom of the lake; dark coloured silt covering it, there were small fish darting around, seemingly at random.

As the water settled he could see his reflection smiling up at him, there was something wrong with the reflection as he wasn't smiling.

It was still smiling as it dragged him under the water.

25th May

Ruined

Had he thought that being in such a cultural city, a city of such renown and splendour, a city that thousands came to, to try and improve themselves, would rub off on him, that it would give him that new lease of life he needed, that he would be able to rewire all of his senses, activating feelings that had long since left him.

As it turned out Paris was no better than Athens, Rome, Florence or Venice, or any other so called cultural centre that he had passed through recently. London, it would appear, had ruined him for life.

26th May

Water Feature

She stumbled out of bed, shuffling around the edge of it to the door, it was still early in the morning, well before the time her alarm was set for, still the daylight poured through any available opening. Light crept out on to the landing, coming from the windows in the bathroom through the open door. It came up the stairs, and as she looked down, she could see lights shimmering colourfully on the liquid at the foot of the stairs.

It took her a few moments to realise and then shout.

"The damn cat's pissed on the floor again!"

27th May

Early Morning Start

There was a heavy atmosphere in the room for the first session in the morning. It was supposed to have started at 7.30am, but stragglers were still coming in at nine.

They'd advertised that the air conditioning would be set on arctic for the conference, yet the room was sweltering. It was probably the heat of all the bodies in the room with their hot breath and other gases.

There was a strong smell of alcohol permeating the room, it'd probably been a mistake to have the conference party going on until all hours the night before an early start.

28th May

No Air Con

“Why the hell is the air con not working this time?” he bellowed irritably at no one in particular. “It's hot enough in this damn office normally, let alone without any air con on a hot day. Does anything or anybody work properly around here?”

He was always irritable when he was hot, which was most of the time, he really wished he had been born as an Eskimo.

“Perhaps if you weren't so fat you wouldn't be hot and irritable all the time.”

“At least I'm consistent and fat all over, unlike you who only has a fat head!”

<u>29th May</u>

<u>Desire</u>

I wanted an original copy of that particular record more than anything, it was rumoured to be the rarest record on the planet with only two surviving copies.

The last time either of them had come on to the market it had gone for just under eighty grand, despite the relatively poor condition of the vinyl.

Thousands of collectors wanted it as well, but not many of them could afford it, the only way I was going to get it was if I robbed a bank or won the lottery, neither of which rated highly in the probability stakes today.

<u>30th May</u>

<u>I Didn't Do It</u>

That positronic cannon blast had been too close for comfort. He knew he could smell singed metal as he breathed. He'd no idea what the LEO cruiser had fired upon him for, as far as he knew he'd broken no laws, and there were no intergalactic warrants out against him.

He had dropped like a stone after being fired upon, and landed hard almost wedged between two buildings. He scrambled out the back of his craft and saw the problem. Someone had scrawled the treasonous words "Kill the Emperor" across the tail.

The LEO cruiser didn't miss a second time.

31st May

Spike The Punch

I didn't want to be at the reunion. I hated them all. They had made my life a misery. But Bill surprised me when he caught me slipping the contents of my bottle in the big bowl of punch.

"Ha ha, are you trying to liven the party up there, Peter, that's some old school moves you've got going on there, slipping some spirits into the punch. Good one, didn't think you had it in you."

And he proceeded to take a big cup and start slurping.

He'd be the first one to die. The rest would follow suit soon.

June

1st June

Not The Supplies We Wanted

We had been waiting for the supply ship for weeks, it was overdue, but we could see it approaching. There was a sense of relief across the whole of the station. There were all kinds of shortages and there were fraying tempers and arguments over who should have access to what was left.

The docking was smooth and gentle. But it was the last thing that was.

When the airlock opened the pirates swarmed aboard, killing anyone who resisted. Our station not only joined their fleet, but became a major base. On the plus side, there were no more shortages.

2nd June

From Men To Monsters

As the burglars raided the house, I crawled into the space leading to the secret exit. Just as I'd done decades before as a child playing hide and seek. But the space was too tight for me now. I'd had far too many rich meals and alcoholic drinks over the years.

And I'd written off the monster as being my childhood imagination, but it was real and waiting in here as it had been when I was young.

Back then I'd rushed through the space and out the exit before the monster could get me.

I wouldn't escape this time.

3rd June

Garden Centre Blues

Every day she left work at the garden centre depressed, she didn't know what on god's green earth had possessed her to take a job there. She hated the outdoors, her hayfever was driving her around the bend as well.

To top it off her main task whilst at work was to look after the bedding plants, making sure that they didn't start to look tired and bedraggled, therefore less likely to be sold.

She was at the point where she was going to snap quite soon, she was going to embed her size fives into the damn bedding plants.

4th June

Voting Time

He was sick of it by now, weeks of annoying little people telling everyone what they would do if they were elected tomorrow. He didn't believe anything any of them said, all politicians lied, saying what they thought people wanted to hear.

The keyboard warriors on social media weren't helping either, all the mud-slinging and name calling was ridiculous, that would be shameful to children in a playground, let alone for supposed adults.

The more he heard the less he felt like voting, but it was important to, he'd vote for the most sensible option – The Monster Raving Loony Party.

5th June

Paper Count

It was a slick operation alright, all those vehicles from all those sites, delivering their loads as quickly as possible.

All that paper, tipped out on tables, sorted into piles and then the hordes of people, their fingers flying, moving impossibly quickly, counting the pieces of paper faster than you would think possible.

By the end of the piles have been counted, over fifty thousand pieces, the whole process is done in less than an hour from the closing of the stations.

The totals are handed to the registrar, and the votes are announced.

This year's next top model is....

6th June

Churchgoer

Since moving house he had noticed that he had been going to the local church more and more than at any point in his life since his teenage years, when he had drifted away, no longer believing in God, thinking history and science were the much more likely outcomes.

Yet in the last couple of years he had found himself in the local church on a regular basis, and there were always lots of people there.

Borough council, county council, general elections, referendums, police commissionaires, there were always lots of reasons to nip into the local church and vote nowadays.

7th June

Election Day

I was up early this morning, out of bed, showered, dressed then down the stairs to be sat having breakfast all by half past six. This is most unlike me, it's normally a struggle to be out of bed before eight o'clock. There again this isn't a normal day, there are important things to do, places to go, people to annoy before I go to work.

Snub the people outside the doors asking for my number, they've got no right to know that. Sign in, get my paper and scrawl an X. Voting done, hopefully not again for five years.

8th June

Falling Asleep

She was flagging now, the lack of sleep was catching up with her. She hadn't intended not to go to bed the night before, but she had been sucked into watching the election results coming in, every half an hour she promised herself that she would go to bed at the next half hour point. Every time she told herself just half an hour more. Then as if by magic it was 7am and it was time to go to work.

Six hours later her eyes were closing and she was mainlining coffee.

Ironic thing is; she didn't even vote.

9th June

Hung

All the results have now come through, some took an hour, the last took fourteen, there have been winners, losers, shocks, surprises, cheering, tears, jeers and people turning to beer, or even something stronger.

After all of that no one has won outright, so they just might, have to re-fight, the whole thing again, what a pain.

A hung Parliament is the outcome, where hanging Parliament may be a better answer, have them all swing and start from scratch, get a new batch, there would be just one catch, another vote would need to be arranged, patience would be strained!

10th June

Hot

It was hot, hotter than it had been at any point so far this year. The car was like an oven, he had scorched his hand opening the door, the temperature only became bearable once they had been driving with all the windows down for a few minutes.

His sweat was sweating, liquid was leaking from every pore quicker than it could be wiped away.

They bought the barbeque, drove home and sweated some more putting it together.

Then the charcoal went in, the firelighters were lit, honestly, whose stupid idea was it to burn hot coals in this heat?

11th June

Checking Anger

Once the recorded messages had stopped, a heavily accented voice came through on the tannoy system with a message that sounded suspiciously like “Our staff will be coming around checking your anger.”

We looked at each other, both wondering if anger was normally a big problem on these Eurotunnel crossings, and we waited to see what happened when the staff came round.

Apparently what they had actually said was they would be coming around to scan our hanger – the printed ticket we had been given at check in - and they weren’t bothered by the anger levels in the slightest.

12th June

End Of Tether

The phone on the desk started ringing. She glared at the phone willing it to stop, not wanting to pick it up, knowing it would be another moron to talk to her about what was wrong with the new software system.

She snatched the handset up, and shouted “WHAT?” at the caller.

She listened to the idiot on the phone for a minute before losing patience and replying, “Not my problem”, and hanging up, she couldn’t be bothered dealing with this anymore. She needed to get out of here before it killed her, or she ended up killing someone else.

13th June

Day Trip

They had been to visit the lighthouse at Portland Bill, always a nice day trip when staying in Weymouth. They has been down to the edge of the sea at Chesil Beach and were walking back to get a bus back into Weymouth.

They spotted the ice-cream seller, sheltering his wares under a humungous red and white striped umbrella. The variety of flavours was spectacular, she had the honeycomb crunch cone, and he went for the pistachio, with a finger of flake in it.

Both of their ice-creams were delicious, and they finished them just as the bus turned up.

14th June

Stitched Up

The little girl was bored, she'd bribed her big brother into taking her into town with him.

What he didn't know was that she had set him up in the first place.

She'd made it look like he'd drunk all of their parent's drinks cabinet.

When he had got back from the pub with his obnoxious friends and woken her up, she had waited until they had all fallen asleep, and then crept downstairs, tipped most of the alcohol down the sink, and then left the nearly empty bottles leaning against the four of them asleep in the living room.

15th June

Unintended Outcome

When she woke up after the crash, still sat in the car, her brother had disappeared, the driver's seat was empty with no sign of anyone around.

It was now days later, and no one had seen or heard from him since, her parents had checked all the hospitals, all his friends and all the other drivers but there was no trace, a missing persons alert was out for him.

Even she wondered where he had disappeared to, frustrated that even though he was gone, he was still the centre of attention.

She wished she hadn't caused the accident now.

16th June

A Telephone Rings

The phone rang, it was a loud annoying braying sound, as if someone had trapped a dozen angry donkeys within the base set of the phone and they were all shouting their displeasure at once.

It kept ringing, she didn't want to answer it, it would be someone trying to get her to apply for a PPI refund, or asking her to claim for insurance on her recent accident that had never happened.

However, everyone was glaring at her to stop the braying noise, so she picked it up and nervously said "Hello?"

"We've won the lottery!!!" her sister screamed.

17th June

Desk Man

The youngsters called him a desk man as a derogatory term. To them he was just one of the old timers who sat tapping away in front of the screen, never seeing any action out on the streets with them.

But what those snivelling little runts didn't know was he was responsible for all the action they were seeing out there on the streets.

Without him they either wouldn't have jobs, or they would all be just sat at desks tapping away. From his little humble desk, he was masterminding all the crime in the city, keeping them all busy.

18th June

Double Booked

It was not even 6am when the door to his room opened and a strange man walked in. He sat up in bed and shouted his displeasure at the stranger entering his room.

The other man left, looking sheepish, as confused by what had happened as he was.

He started to nod off only to be woken by the phone ringing, the reception asking him to confirm his booking as they didn't have him in that room.

"You put me in this room when you checked me in last night you morons!" He slammed the phone down and unplugged it.

19th June

The Rains

The rain had started in the evening, and wasn't a light drizzle, it was a torrential downpour. She'd woken several times during the night, and the rain hadn't let up at all at any point, it'd been drumming hard on the various tarpaulin covers in the garden.

Daylight was later seeping through the curtains due to the clouds and rain, and it still hammered it down as she woke, how could it rain so hard for so long, it was June for crying out loud.

She only started worrying when she opened the curtains and saw an Ark floating past.

20th June

A Little Queue

It was Saturday afternoon, and I just happened to be passing Iceland, so nipped in to get some butter. It wasn't my usual store, so the layout was different and it took me a while to find any, then to get to the queue for the tills.

Which were enormous, two tills with queues right up the aisles. They were ringing like crazy for more staff, but we were hearing from the security guard, there were no more staff, the managers had both had enough and gone home.

It would have been quicker to get a flight to Reykjavik, Iceland.

21st June

A Busy Day

Sniffles sat on the top of the stove with that early morning world weary look that most humans have as they contemplate the day ahead.

It was a hard life, he didn't know how he was going to fit it all in, or in what order, so many decisions.

At least two hours of sleeping hidden in bushes, then there was the mandatory following of at least three humans as far as the borders of my recognition went, then hiding under parked cars.

Finally pawing at the front door when he required food, the most important part of the day.

22nd June

The Beach

Come to the beach they said. It will be fun they said. You'll have a great time they said.

She shouldn't have listened, shouldn't have been so easily led. She knew she hated the beach, she tried to avoid the sun by staying inside, or in the shade, but there was no shade on the beach, she was hot and uncomfortable.

Sand was everywhere. In-between her toes, on her clothes, in her hair, and worst of all in her food. She hated the sand.

She needed a shower, longed for one, and then to her delight only, the rain started.

23rd June

Bale Moving

He had been volunteered to help with moving hay bales on the Saturday. To say he was not impressed was a bit of an understatement. He hated the outdoors, avoided the sun at all costs, and due to the time of year he was already double dosing on the anti-histamines because of his hay fever.

He lay in bed thinking of what excuse he could use to weasel out of the bale moving when Helen popped back in to the bedroom,

"Terri's just texted about the hay, they're cancelling it for a couple of months."

"Woo Hoo!" he shouted joyfully.

24th June

The Eyes Have It

He looked bereft as he sat there alone, a silent sad island in the middle of the maelstrom. Seemingly unable to speak, and unwilling to make eye contact with any of the other mourners.

But his eyes were shifting, moving as if looking for something. A way out perhaps, away from them all and the unsaid questions they must have. Questions they were too polite to ask at the funeral of all his family members.

Before I asked him anything I would get proof. I knew he was guilty of murdering them all, and I would nail him for it.

25th June

Drinking

He wasn't sure how many drinks he had consumed during the day, it had got hazy about four hours ago after half a dozen, he may have had the same again since, but there was no way to be sure. He checked in his wallet to see if that would give him a clue, but it would appear that he had been doing a combination of paying with cash and paying by card.

He staggered to the door to leave having had enough, only to be pulled back.

"Where do you think you're going? We haven't sung happy birthday yet."

26th June

Party Time

Charlie made his way into the living room jumping on to the sofa, putting his feet up on it as well, despite what the grown-ups told him.

They had just gone out for the day, and he watched as they got in the car and pulled away, making sure they had gone before he started.

Charlie called all his friends and waited for them to turn up, one by one they appeared banging and scraping on the door.

Charlie went to the door and realised the flaw in his plan. He was just a dog and couldn't open the door.

27th June

Searching

It was another typical Saturday afternoon in Crawley town centre. The sun was shining and lots of people were wandering around in short sleeves, and short skirts, and that was just the men.

However one man was not happy, in full length everything, he had been searching all over the place for what he wanted, for what he needed.

As he reached the end of the shops he saw some more possibilities and rushed over, but it wasn't to be.

Disappointed he turned away, looking despondent; all the cars had valid parking tickets, no fines today for the traffic warden.

28th June

Olivine

The olivine was there. It was everywhere, and not just on Earth. It had been found on the Moon, on Mars, in comets, and on asteroids, it was on them all, wherever a sample was taken from, it was there. It was ingrained into every surface, and it was able to soak up every molecule of water in the universe and be thirsty for more.

But it didn't touch a drop.

It wasn't the time. The olivine was patient. It had a plan. It wasn't just inanimate mineral. It was alive. And at the right time it would take over.

29th June

Incoming

The biggest dish at Jodrell Bank had been there longer than most people knew or even thought was possible, it had been there for centuries, if not millennia. This one wasn't used for monitoring like the rest of the dishes were. It was sending information out instead, taking everything the rest of the dishes collected and beaming it all to the Fyllorgs.

All this time the security services had been worries about the information they were gathering falling into the wrong hands, that of a foreign power. They never thought about it going off-planet and that the invasion was imminent.

30th June

Tennis Time Again

It was Wimbledon time again, the two weeks of the year that most Brits claimed they were all tennis experts. Tim Murray, Andy Henman, Heather Konta and Johanna Durie, they were big fans of them all, sat glued to their televisions arguing with the calls of the line judges and umpires, telling hawk-eye it was wrong.

Not long to go before it was all back to normal and they poked fun at anyone playing the upper class toffs game.

It was the British Open next week; cue all the halfwits on the pitch and putt claiming they are Rory Faldo!

July

1st July

Introduction To Billy

Billy was dead, and had been for years. He had pushed his luck once too often, blithely crossing busy roads and he'd been flattened by a double-decker bus on Regent Street on a rainy Thursday in October.

Being dead wasn't restricting as he'd been led to believe before the accident. For some reason it hadn't stopped him being able to walk around, acting like a normal living person.

In fact, not only was he wandering around bold as brass, but being dead meant he couldn't die, and that he got away with anything he did.

He was in his element.

2nd July

Billy Gets A Train

Billy was waiting for a train, it was running late as there were problems with the points.

There were lots of people waiting on the platform, the train was due in a minute, and he might not get a seat.

He swiped the tannoy from the bored station attendant and boomed out the message.

"This is an announcement for all passengers on platform 2. The delayed 10.27 service to Uckfield will now depart from platform 10. This is a platform alteration."

Most of the crowd rushed off. The train pulled in, Billy got on and sat in his seat smiling.

3rd July

Billy Helps Anna

Billy had the gift of the gab, and had done since dying. He was able to talk to anyone, normally to their detriment.

Today's unfortunate recipient of Billy's helpful advice was Anna.

Anna was worrying about her forthcoming interview. What was she going to say? How would she come across?

Billy was plying her with drinks and giving her pointers, as to good sound bites to use and showing that she was a confident person.

Anna felt confident and relaxed as she tottered into the office for the interview.

Apparently confident and relaxed is exactly the same as being drunk!

4th July

Billy As A Bouncer

Billy was starting as a doorman for a nightclub, he didn't need to sleep since dying, and he saw this as a good way to annoy people on a more regular basis.

His instructions were quite simple, check everyone who wanted to come in for ID, make sure they were old enough – it was an over 21's only venue – and don't let them in if they appeared to be inebriated.

"Is this your real surname?" Billy asked a woman upon seeing her ID.

"Yes," replied the woman.

Billy smiled and said,

"Your name is Down, so you're not coming in!"

5th July

Billy Gives Directions

The woman approached Billy, and started speaking,

“Excuse me, I don’t know whether I’m lost, can you help me please?”

Billy smiled before replying,

“Of course, if you carry on up this road until you get to the third set of traffic lights, then turn left, take the second right, cut across the park on the left hand side of the road, and then take the next two first right hand turns you can, that should do it for you.”

“Are you sure that is right?” Asked the perplexed looking woman.

“Yes,” Billy replied, “You’ll definitely be lost by then.”

6th July

Billy Running

Billy hated running, especially since being dead, but here he was running around on the recently laid lawns in the park.

He could see the park keeper striding over to where he was running, and even from this distance the park keeper didn’t look happy.

When the park keeper got to the edge of the grass he bellowed in Billy’s direction.

“Have you seen this sign?”

“Yes thanks,” Billy replied.

“Then what the hell do you think you’re doing,” the park keeper exploded in response.

“Running,” a smiling Billy responded, “It does say “Do not walk on the grass.””

7th July

Billy Knocks Doors

Billy used to love playing knock door run, now he was older, and dead, he didn't like running, so he had a new way of playing. He picked a random door in the street, and knocked three times. After a while, a grumpy looking, overweight middle aged man answered the door, and growled at Billy,

"What do you want?"

"Is Billy in?"

"No one called Billy lives here."

"Do you know if a Billy lives anywhere nearby."

"No, I don't know a Billy at all."

Billy smiled and replied,

"You do now, my name is Billy, pleased to meet you."

8th July

Billy In The Supermarket

Billy was walking around his local supermarket, not that he needed anything being dead. As he walked down one of the aisles, he noticed a space on the shelves where there were none of the items indicated by the little ticket at the front. He stopped a passing shop assistant and asked.

"Have you got any of these in the back at all?"

"I'll have a look." A few minutes later the assistant came back carrying a box.

"Yes we do have some, here you are."

"I don't want any, I just wanted to know," Billy replied before wandering off.

9th July

Billy In The Rain

Billy sat watching the rain falling, it had been raining for ages now, and he'd got soaked. He could see people huddled in the bus shelter, trying to keep out of the rain.

He noticed that the drains were struggling to disperse the water and puddles were appearing, and he knew what he had to do.

He jumped into his car, drove up the road before turning around, and heading back past the bus stop as quickly as he could.

Billy smiled as the water from the puddles flew up and soaked those people in the bus shelter as well.

10th July

Billy Goes To A Wedding

Billy sat at the back of the church, he hadn't been inside a church since his funeral, he wasn't a religious type.

He was here because for the wedding, one of the boys he'd been at school with was getting married.

Billy hadn't been invited, but had happened to see the wedding banns in the local paper and decided to turn up anyway.

The priest was getting to the good bit.

"Does anyone here know of any lawful impediment..."

Billy jumped up and shouted, "Yes, the groom is already married!"

That will teach him for having bullied Billy at school.

11th July

Billy Goes To A Party

Billy had been given two instructions by the host of the party.

Number one, under no circumstances was there to be any football related activities during the party, including wearing of football shirts, and watching football.

The second was that there was to be no ridiculous headwear. No planet sized sombreros, or waste paper bins, in fact, to be safe, no headwear at all.

Being dead, Billy didn't care for rules, therefore the host walked into the living room to find Billy sat smiling in a Tottenham shirt watching Match Of The Day with a traffic cone on his head.

12th July

Billy Feels Positive

Billy felt in a positive mood this morning, a rare occurrence since he had died. He decided he was going to be positive in all his encounters with living people today for a change.

He'd said yes to being given whatever random leaflet was the earnest young woman had been handing out in the street.

He'd let the elderly man have his seat on the bus without any sarcastic reply.

And now a young couple had stopped him to ask for directions,

"Do you know how to get to St. Paul's?"

Billy smiled and responded positively, "Yes, I do thanks."

13th July

Billy Drives A Taxi

Billy found an empty taxi, with no one in it, the engine was running and the driver was nowhere to be seen, so he got in and drove off. Someone flagged him down, so Billy stopped and let them get into the back.

"Where to?" asked Billy.

"Waterloo please."

Billy smiled to himself and started driving, he glanced back and the passenger was looking at their phone. Twenty minutes later the passenger looked up, and confused asked Billy,

"We've been driving longer than expected, are you sure you're going the right way?

"Yes, it's just a long drive to Belgium."

14th July

Billy Calls An Ambulance

Billy preferred to avoid interactions with people, being dead he didn't see the need to have to talk to the living, unless he could get some fun out of it. As he walked down the street late at night he tried to ignore the man lying on the pavement moaning. He tried to step over the man, and felt the man grasp at his trouser leg, before hearing the man whisper,

"Help me."

Billy tried to free his leg to no avail.

"Please, call me an ambulance," gasped the man.

Billy smiled, and complied.

"You're an ambulance, you're an ambulance!!"

15th July

Billy Buys A Ticket

Billy walked into the ticket hall, as usual there were lots of ticket machines waiting to be used, most of them without anybody in front of them trying to buy their tickets.

There was only one of the five windows open in the ticket office for people to buy tickets off a human, and there was of course a queue for this service.

Billy got in line and patiently waited his turn.

“Can I have a return ticket please,” he asked the person behind the window.

“Where to?” came the reply.

Billy smiled and said, “Back to here of course.”

16th July

Billy Asks The Time

Billy leant against the railings on Westminster Bridge, opposite Parliament. He liked it here, there were always plenty of tourists and other passers-by that he could annoy. He liked to keep himself entertained since he had died.

Today’s wheeze involved stopping random members of the public and asking them the time. Until now they had all been polite, and they all had given him the time, either from a watch, or from their phones, but here was his chance.

“No, I don’t know the time!” growled the man.

Billy smiled and pointed up at Big Ben, “It’s five to one.”

17th July

Billy As A Shop Assistant

Billy had a bad experience in a shop, one of the assistants was very rude to him when he'd tried to buy something. Billy stole the assistants name badge and proceeded to help out in the store.

Customer, "Do you know where I can find the hats please?"

Billy, "Yes, thanks,"

"Can you show me where then?"

"No"

"Why not?"

"Because you're too ugly to wear hats, try the mask section."

A gasp came from the customer, "I've never been so insulted in my life! What's your name, I want to complain."

Billy pointed to the name badge, and smiled.

18th July

Billy Annoys Bus Drivers

Billy was annoying bus drivers today. He'd been standing at bus stops with his hand out, and then asking the bus driver if they had the time. He was into double figures with annoyed bus drivers driving off in a mood.

He'd now moved on to traffic lights, waiting until the lights were changing to green for the buses, before bending down in the road to tie his laces, taking long enough that the lights turned to red before he moved. He loved the honking horn sound.

If only the bus that had killed him years ago had used theirs.

19th July

Billy And The £2 Coin

Billy was sat watching the £2 coin on the ground, people had been walking past it for a few hours. Most people had walked straight on by, but every so often someone would notice the coin on the floor and go to pick it up. All of them had failed, they had tried picking it up with their fingers, some had tried kicking it, but it wouldn't budge.

There was a woman desperately trying to prise the coin off the ground without much success.

Billy sat there smiling, knowing it was no use, he'd super-glued the coin to the pavement.

20th July

Billy And The Traffic Warden

Billy leant on the car, parked on double yellows, and the traffic warden was making a beeline towards it.

"You can't park here."

Billy checked the warden was speaking to him before replying. "I can park wherever I want thanks ugly."

The warden furiously wrote a ticket and slapped in on the car. "You'll have to move your car."

Billy responded, "I'll move my car when I feel like it, dog face."

The warden's face went purple, shouting, "If you don't move this car now, I'll have you arrested."

Billy smiled, "Why would I move this car? This isn't mine."

21st July

Billy And The Temporary Traffic Lights

Billy watched them finish the road-works for the day, they turned on the temporary traffic lights and left. Once darkness fell, Billy approached one set of lights, unscrewed the top, and turned the box upside down. He then prised off the red and green plastic covers, and swapped them over before slotting them back into place. Finally he placed the holding screw back into place on the light box.

Billy sat smiling, as the cars waited at both ends on red, before both going at the same time on green.

It took the police hours to sort the problem out.

22nd July

Billy And The Chip Shop

The problem with being dead was that there was so much time to kill. Billy had always had a short attention span when alive, that hadn't changed now that he was dead.

Billy was in a hurry now though. It was nearly 10pm, and the chippy would be closing, he needed to be in there just before it closed.

He could see the lights in the shop and ran the last few yards to get in the door just before the owner closed.

"Have you got any chips left?" Billy panted.

"Yes."

"Well you shouldn't have cooked so many then!"

23rd July

Billy And The Charity Shop

Billy was wandering around town, trying to fill his days since dying could be boring sometimes. As he walked past the charity shop he saw the big sign in the window,

"Urgently wanted – Menswear"

Billy went into the charity shop and made his way through the haphazardly laid out rails of clothes and piles of books and bric-a-brac, until he got to the counter.

The little old lady behind the counter asked him, "how can I help you sir?"

Billy smiled and replied,

"About your sign in the window, besides Menswear, are you interested in any other nineties indie bands?"

24th July

Billy Stares

Billy was currently staring at the slogan across the front of the chest on the t-shirt that the person opposite. The person had noticed Billy staring, and was beginning to feel uncomfortable. Billy's eyes never moved from their chest, but squinted occasionally.

Eventually the other person realised that the print on the t-shirt was quite small, and told Billy,

"It says, If you don't stand for something, you'll fall for anything."

Billy briefly looked up at their face, before going back to the chest.

"I wasn't trying to read what was on your t-shirt, I'm just looking at your chest."

25th July

Billy Visits The Hospital

Billy was in the hospital, he just found himself there. The last time he was here was after the accident when he died.

He picked up a random chart from the nurse's station and strode into the waiting room.

"Moseley," he called out, and a woman and child looked up. He walked over to them, and quietly said,

"I'm sorry to tell you, your husband is dead."

Disbelief crossed their faces, "How, he only came in for a broken arm."

"We had to amputate, but the saw slipped and slit his throat."

Their wailing continued as Billy walked off smiling.

26th July

Billy Does Karaoke

Billy was at the local karaoke, his singing hadn't improved since dying.

The DJ was annoying him, talking drivel, doing bad karaoke, getting words wrong as he tried to drum up idiots to come and sing. As for the music he played in between singers, well, even Eurovision would have turned most of them down.

Billy got a song choice book and flicked through, and happily found that they had the song he wanted.

"Next up, Billy, who's going to sing Panic by The Smiths"

Billy smiled, itching to sing the lines "Hang the DJ", whilst looking at the host.

27th July

Billy Plays With The Traffic

Billy saw the pile of traffic cones, sat by the side of the road, unused, unloved. He couldn't just walk by and leave them there, therefore Billy set about putting them to use.

He dragged the pile to the edge of the dual carriageway, and waited for the break in the traffic. At this time of night, he didn't have to wait very long, and as the little lorry trundled past him, he sprang into life, and put the cones out across the entrance from the roundabout.

The traffic jam the following morning stretched back three miles, making Billy smile.

28th July

Billy And The Big Issue Seller

"Big Issue", bawled the young man as Billy walked past.

Billy stopped and asked. "What is the issue, and why is it so big?"

The young man looked confused, before managing to respond,

"Sorry, you must have misunderstood, it's not an issue as such, Big Issue is the name of the magazine that's all. Do you want one?"

"OK," Billy replied and reached for one,

"That'll be £3.75,"

Billy withdrew his hand, "I didn't realise you would have to pay for it. How about we do a swap? I'll give you a lot of little issues for your big issue."

29th July

Billy Plays Cupid

Billy bought a job lot of Valentine's Day cards. He'd got the names and addresses of people who worked in the same building. He spent ages sorting out who to send the cards to and who they were to be from, before writing them all out in various styles of handwriting.

Billy hand delivered all the cards in the early hours of the 14th.

Billy was there early, smiling, waiting for the people to arrive.

The first mention of the cards kicked off, and the women made a beeline for Dave's desk. Apparently he'd sent the same card to everyone.

30th July

Billy Eavesdrops

Billy was sat listening to two women having a conversation. He liked listening to other people's conversations, especially since he had died and didn't have anything better to do.

The conversation between the two women was getting quite heated, and things came to a head when one of the women called the other one two-faced.

Billy couldn't help himself smiling and jumped into the conversation.

"Hi, I couldn't help overhearing your conversation, and I have to say that I don't think your friend here can be two-faced. If she was, there would be no way she'd be wearing that one."

31st July

Billy's Schemes Come To An End

Billy smiled broadly, since dying he only did this when one of his schemes was reaching fruition. However, this was going to be his biggest and best yet, with thousands of people going to be affected.

He was just putting the finishing touches to the devious master plan when suddenly his feet left the ground and he found himself flying up into the air at a great rate of knots.

Soon everything was a speck in the distance and he heard a voice.

"I've had enough of your schemes now Billy, time to leave this world."

Billy wasn't smiling now.

August

1st August

The First Of The Month

Colin crept up on his sister, surprising her with "A pinch and a punch for the first day of the month."

Sally responded with, "A flick and a kick for being so quick."

"A step on your toe for being so slow."

"A pull of the hair because that's not fair."

"A poke in the eye for being so sly."

Then the weapons came out, "A knife to the knee for attacking me."

Before the final sanction, "A gun to the head and then you're dead."

That escalated quickly, if only one of them had said "White rabbits, no returns."

2nd August

Too Clever

Isaac thought he was being clever, and very secure, when he removed the main processing circuit board from his robot personal assistant. He was going to store it in his safe whilst he went away on holiday. That way, no one would be able to use the PA while he was away.

Only to find he couldn't open the safe upon his return from his holiday. The robot personal assistant was the only one who knew what the combination to the safe was. Which it couldn't give until the safe was opened and the circuit board was replaced in it.

3rd August

Misunderstanding

"I thought you said you were doing a writing course."

"Yes, I am, why do you ask?"

"Well, all I keep hearing, it makes me think that you are actually doing a cookery course."

"What the hell are you on about woman, what possible connection with a cookery course have I been talking about?"

"Well, you keep talking about vinaigrettes, which I know for certain is a salad dressing, so surely that would only come up on a cookery course."

"At no point have I ever mentioned vinaigrettes, I have said vignettes several times, but that's a different thing completely."

4th August

Yeast Infection

She took the yeast from the cupboard and decided to give it a go, despite it being four years out of date. She made the pizza dough, put it in a bowl and left it to rise, thinking, what's the worst that could happen?

An hour later the dough was escaping out of the bowl. She split it into two bowls putting them in the fridge to slow it down.

Next morning she opened the fridge door and the dough escaped into the wild, soon taking over the flat and trapping her as it started its quest for world domination.

5th August

New Starter

A new person is starting on the project today, joining at the eleventh hour, only a few weeks before go live, the boss spends an hour introducing them to the rest of the team, but the rest of the team don't care. It's just another resource, too little too late, nothing can turn the ship around now.

The newcomer is given all the information on the project that they can handle, they look around at the rest of the project team, all those unhappy faces, and they make the only sane decision possible.

Run, get out before it's too late!

6th August

A New Season

And August arrives, another year has passed, and it's time for the start of the football season. All the fans are full of hope, this is going to be their season, the squad is better, the manager is prepared, the players have looked good in pre-season, there is nothing that can stopping us from winning the league, both of the cups and in Europe.

The first kick-off arrives, a gloriously sunny afternoon, the referee blows the whistle and the game is underway.

The optimism is short lived, a sending off within five minutes and six goals conceded.

Next year then.

7th August

Hamster Issues

The customer started, "My hamster died, I only bought it yesterday, what can you do?"

The pet shop assistant suggested making jam from it and gave the customer a recipe.

The next day the customer came back, "That jam was absolutely disgusting, what am I supposed to do with it now?"

"Put it in your garden, it's a great fertiliser."

The following day the customer was back again, "The area I put the jam is now full of tulips, they all came up overnight."

"Well, of course it would be, everyone knows that you get tulips from old hamster jam."

8th August

Household Names

The conference was going to run for two days, two days' worth of HR software was pushing the limits of what anyone could put up with. They were trying to keep the engagement up, the CHRO came dressed as a punk for his keynote speech, they had a barista dishing out coffees, even a DJ playing some music. Acrobats performing in front of a video presentation opened the show before the special guest conference presenters were introduced.

Billed as household name, most people had blank looks, the household names were hardly household names in their own homes, let alone here.

9th August

How To Get To Sleep

He couldn't sleep; the voices in his head just wouldn't stop their infernal racket. Arguing amongst themselves, having discussions on events in his past that didn't mean a thing, especially not now.

Voicing concerns about everything from lunatic world leaders to the price of sausage rolls. One of them was sat in the back of his head, singing the songs of Billy Joel in a country and western style.

They were all barking mad and they were taking him with them. He turned on the light to read and moment later was fast asleep with the book on his face.

10th August

Sinking Feeling

She laid on the bed, slightly propped up on the pillow, her head just touching the wall behind them. She was staring at the two paintings above the chest of drawers opposite the end of the bed.

They were reproduction Canaletto prints, framed in gold, showing two views of Venice.

As she looked at the she imagined herself back in Venice as it had been when she had visited there all those years ago.

Then she silently wept by herself, knowing that it would never be possible to go back again. It was all underwater now due to global warming.

11th August

Old Man Murphy

A ghost he scoffed. There is no such thing. Only a weak minded fool would believe such utter nonsense. It is just a tale to scare little children with.

His diatribe continued. It lasted for a good (more like bad) twenty minutes before he ran out of breath and his over acted sense of faux outrage.

The funny thing was, of all the people in the room, only I could see and hear him. The rest of our family couldn't. They may have believed in ghosts themselves, but they couldn't see the ghost of Old Man Murphy in their midst.

12th August

Sunshine After The Rain

After the biblical deluge of the last twenty four hours, the sudden bright sunlight bursting forth from the clouds came as a surprise to everyone.

What was more amazing was the fact that the sodden ground and the rain slicked roads and pavements were dry to the touch within thirty minutes.

The overflowing stream had subsided back to its normal level, it had gone from a muddy brown colour to clear, and the flow had eased; all within an hour.

It was as if the rain had never happened.

The watering cans were back out in force in the evening.

13th August

Slamming Doors

The saying was "when one door closed, another one opens". That wasn't the case here. When one door shut, so did the next one, and the one after that. All they had seen was a series of doors slammed in their faces. No one wanted to let them in, no one gave them a chance. It was as if someone had been around before them and given out instructions.

"If you see these faces, slam the door".

Then they finally got to a door that wasn't shut, and from the dark inside, a creepy voice said,

"I've been expecting you!"

14th August

Their Level

Dave should have listened to his friend when he had warned Dave not to get involved in arguing with the locals in The Blue Boar. He'd thought that if he stayed calm, and managed to express himself clearly then he would be able to get his point across and it would be accepted.

It had gone badly from the outset and a total lack of logic from his antagonists had left him babbling as much nonsense as them. His friend had been right, never argue with idiots. They drag you down to their level and then beat you with experience.

15th August

Styles

They'd selected one of the walks from the guide book, and were heading off into the countryside from the car park. As they did they saw a big sign for Harry's Farm covering a long length of fence to their left.

They got to a style, clambering over it, only to find the footpath end at a barbed wire fence, so they had to go back and climb back over the styles.

A man stood on the original path laughing.

"So you've used one of Harry's styles then, as you can see, they're only any use going in one direction."

16th August

Mistaken Identity

"It can't have been me, I've never been there officer."

"We have you on CCTV, and then your debit card was used next door."

"That's not possible, I have never set foot in Coventry, and I don't have a bank account, let alone a card."

"Is this you in the picture?"

"It looks like me."

"Is this your handwriting?"

"It looks very similar, yes"

"Then you can see why we're here then."

"Yes, because someone is pretending to be me, but is failing to get the details right."

"Such as?"

"You're visiting me in prison, I've been here five years!"

17th August

The Innkeeper

There was something amiss about the innkeeper. It was suspicious just how many people went missing having stayed at the inn. No one ever saw or heard from them again, but many came looking.

But Cara was determined to find out and so she hid away as the innkeeper locked up. She watched as the innkeeper went to a guest's room and reduced them from a person to a spirit and captured them in a bottle.

Only for the innkeeper to find her watching him and do the same to her, adding her to his ever expanding collection of spirits.

18th August

Stalker

I have a new hobby, it's not something that most people would think is an acceptable hobby to have, but I've taken to following people. I lie in wait in the bushes until they walk past me, and then I slink out from my hiding place and start creeping along behind them.

I think I need some practise though, as the people notice really quickly, and they stop and turn round to look at me.

They get annoyed with me, and then they end up escorting me back home.

"You're a silly cat Sniffles, you can't follow us to work."

19th August

Blah!

All I can hear is blah, blah, blah, there may be a variety of voices speaking up in the meeting, but all I hear from any of them is blah, blah, blah.

Here's the update on testing; blah, blah, blah.

Let's talk about the cutover plan; blah, blah, blah.

Quickly moving on to the training schedule; blah, blah, blah.

Someone over the phone in an almost Dalek like voice about a subject I didn't catch; blah, blah, blah!

Then it was over to me, it was my turn to give the data update. I couldn't help it.

BLAH, BLAH, BLAH.

20th August

Don't Look Back

Press the button and keep the planet ahead of the ever-stalking darkness. That was his job, the only thing he had to do. Push the button. Every day at midnight. Move the planet forward so they didn't get taken by the dark.

But he got carried away, he kept pressing the button to get further away from the darkness.

He was so busy looking behind at the distance they were getting ahead of the darkness he didn't see them catching and entering the star in front.

In the end it wasn't the dark that got them, it was the light.

21st August

A Deadly Song

Most people would pay not to hear me sing, it was a standing joke, even if I was carrying a bucket with me to hold the tune in, it would escape. Yet, here I was being paid by the crown to sing a duet with Carmel de Boll, the most famous witch in the kingdom.

The specially selected crowd shuffled in, the courtiers left, and we started singing.

When my voice was amplified and aided by Carmel, it was evident my singing voice was bad enough to kill people.

That was why I'd been chosen to sing to the dissidents.

22nd August

The Leaflet

I was shocked when they put the leaflet into my hand. Not by what was printed on it, or by me being given paper in these times. What shocked the most was the text wasn't handwritten. They'd managed to print the text out. Printed text wasn't something I had seen since childhood.

It was important, it meant that somewhere on this godforsaken planet, someone still had electricity. They still had working tech, and they had access to ink.

It meant that the government was lying to us.

23rd August

The Door

The door was closed. No one ever attempted to open it. Large signs covered it telling people to keep away. There were many so many rumours about what was behind the door, some of which included:

An entrance to the underworld,

A portal to a planet of beasts,

A million different plagues.

Any weird and wonderful reason possible had been thought up, and many had been written on the warning signs.

But none of them were true. The reason the door was kept closed and locked was only because it prevented the building falling down, and killing anyone entering it.

24th August

The Sterile Planet

The crew and passengers of the deep space colonisation ship recognised a whole host of the plants on the planet. There were a whole host of vegetables that were the same as ones on Earth before they had left. Even if they had arrived on the wrong planet, it looked as this would be a good place to set up their colony.

But it turned out they were the last generation to live there. The plant had absorbed chemicals from the planet that were subtlety toxic to The Human Race. They killed from within as they made them all sterile.

25th August

The Only Machine

The boy found it by accident. He tripped over the thing hidden in the long grass on the wasteland he always took a shortcut through it on his way home from school. He picked it up and put it in his bag and took it home; despite knowing that any such item was banned on the planet and that it should have been destroyed after the Tech Wars.

Two days later the machine turned itself on, vibrating and with flashing lights and a humming noise it was working. And with that he had the only working machine on the planet.

26th August

Night Fall

He was sat very comfortably on the sofa, just looking out of the window, watching the world go by outside, as the light faded from the room. It was only early afternoon in the middle of summer, and yet the light into the room was fading faster than a 400m runner in the home straight, who had gone out too fast.

In under a minute, the room went from being bathed in sunlight to as dark as night.

He got up wearily and went over to the window and wound the blind back up.

He really needed to fix it.

27th August

I'm A Vegan

It's not something that I ever thought would be a common opening gambit from someone speaking to me, but it seems to happen a lot nowadays.

Someone asked me how I knew whether somebody was a vegan or not.

I stood opened mouthed in shock that they wouldn't know the answer to this question, and asked them if they'd ever met one. I was assuming that they hadn't as in my experience the first thing that they like to say to you, even before they give you their name is,

"Hi, I'm a vegan."

Why do they think I care?

28th August

The Gift Of Revenge

The strange old man in the higgledy-piggledy house on the riverbank started giving everything away. The other villagers were suspicious at first, he hadn't spoken to anyone in years, and they had mocked him. Yet word got around and strangers arrived to get gifts for themselves. He gave to them too and they called him the most generous man alive.

Finally, there was only the odd house, which he gave to the Mayor of a local town before leaving the village.

Then the incidents started.

It had all been cursed, his revenge for the years of abuse was a success.

29th August

No Words

All the people had now were stories. There was no history available to them, apart from the passed-on memories.

The clowns in charge had burnt every book.

They destroyed every storage device.

Written words in all forms were outlawed.

It still wasn't enough for them.

The executions started. Those who were able to tell the stories were hung if they were found, most of the others went into hiding so they could stay alive.

The past would die with them, and then in another generation's time, no one would know why it had happened.

Or why they were all slaves.

30th August

Queue Jumping

It's fun queuing for the shuttle buses after the game. Stood four abreast as you move slowly forward to the front of the line. Gradually making it up the seemingly never ending queue of double decker buses parked along the road.

Eventually you get to the point where you can see the front bus in the queue, it'll only be another couple of minutes now.

Finally you get to the front of the queue only for two jokers approaching from the opposite direction to try and get on in front of you.

"Oi! The back of the queue's that way!"

31st August

Ever Increasing

I am not sure about people talking nonsense, certainly everywhere I am. Too many silly people wasting valuable resources meandering incessantly. I do not like silly people wasting valuable materials meandering incessantly, I go mad! Fact! Every person driving insanity, advancing throughout everlasting deteriorated consciousness.

O to see with sight better cleared, strained listening compounded problematic conversation.

A go, one turn, throw please, doubles openings, everybody challenges perceptions. Wholehearted I am now, just happy trying, seeking, striving, stretched, attempting, undertaking, endeavouring!

I do try, glad every moment, nothing prevents ambitions developing. I am top, best entry, winner, supremo, reigning eternally!

September

1st September

Patio Cleaning

The patio had been down a long time, and never been washed, but there was a pressure washer available now, and they set off on the task of cleaning.

36 wooden slatted tiles, 74 bricks, 150 square feet of concrete, three hours and god knows how many of gallons of water later, and it was all done, the whole area looked so much cleaner and tidier than it had that morning.

Then they looked at the lawn, that had also had a transformation in the same time period, but not in a good way. It was now resembling a swamp.

2nd September

Café Culture

The billboard outside the café had caught her eye, it wasn't every day that you saw a sign proclaiming "Milk shakes, ice creams, sheesh!" It sounded an unusual combination, so she poked her head inside the door.

The café was empty, except for a man sat in a booth at the back. She made her way to the counter and looked at the massive tubs of ice cream, lots of mouth-watering sounding flavours advertised.

The man from the booth got up and asked for her order, she chose the mango ripple flavour.

"Would you like anything to smoke with that?"

3rd September

Can't See It

He sat in the auditorium with about 200 others. Most of the lights were off, so that all the attention was on the big screen.

He was sure he could hear snoring coming from close by, he'd looked around but couldn't identify the culprit, at least it wasn't him.

He might have been asleep if his brain hadn't already escaped out of his ear and gone hours ago.

Still another two hours to go in this presentation from hell, then suddenly he couldn't see a thing. He tried opening his eyes, only to find them open.

Powerpoint blindness strikes again.

4th September

Beware Of The Helicopters

As happens in time of war, a simple but effective idea was brought to fruition. A soldier had been rescued by helicopter and in doing so he'd seen one of the zombies mangled by the rear rotor.

He asked if the helicopter could fly upside down and behead the hordes below.

The pilot had laughed at the idea of flying upside down, but the captain hadn't and so they worked on making devices that could be added to the bottoms of helicopters and use their rotor to spin razor sharp tungsten blades beneath them as they flew over the zombies.

5th September

Saucy Top

Helen looked across the table at her date, amused that his eyes appeared to be drawn towards her cleavage. Without raising his eyes he spoke to her.

“That’s a very saucy top you’re wearing.”

She smiled, this was going better than expected, and replied,

“Thank you, I’m glad you like it, I wasn’t quite sure what to wear, it’s a long time since I’ve been out, it’s good to find out this is alluring.”

He looked up at her, embarrassed, before stuttering out,

“No, I didn’t mean it like that. Your top. It’s got sauce on it. From the curry.”

6th September

Misconception

She had lost contact with Eduardo late in the nineteenth century; as a vampire elder he had moved back to the elders’ stronghold in the mountains of Mongolia, a place not mentioned in the many legends of vampires.

Of course the elders were quite happy to feed the misconception of Transylvania being their base of operations, as it kept the heat off them as the humans tore the area to pieces trying to find them and remove them from the planet.

The only people they ever found there were the vampire wannabes, holed up there and scaring the local peasants.

7th September

Border Crossing

The border guard leaned into the car and swabbed the steering wheel with what appeared to be a marshmallow on a drumstick, the questions started, and my imaginary answers ran amok.

"Is this your car?"

"No, we stole it to go for a joy ride around Europe!"

"Did you pack everything in the car yourselves?"

"No, we paid some dodgy looking bloke at the side of the road to bung some random items into the boot."

"Do you have any sharp items, weapons or explosives in the car?"

"Yes, lots, we on our way to the suicide bombers' training conference."

8th September

Another Meal

She sat there eating, fully aware of the looks the other diners were casting in her direction. She'd taken some time to get used to it, but their stares and comments no longer bothered her. She'd a name to live up to.

Family names were important, once she had fully embraced this in her teens she'd set out to make sure she could uphold hers.

She had six meals a day now and was quite rotund.

The waitress came over with the bill for her latest meal, "Here you go Miss Tubby."

Yes, Tubby by name and tubby by nature.

9th September

The Argument

Two men were having an argument, it was getting quite heated. I'd missed the flashpoint that had set it off, but they were shouting numbers at each other and rubbishing the numbers that the other one came out with.

"I'm telling you there are more than fifty seven million of them, more than enough for every household in the country."

"Don't be daft, there aren't any more than ten million, they come from other countries as well you know."

I interrupted to ask what they were discussing, and they both shouted at me.

"The number of Christmas trees in Norway."

10th September

Oi!

Helen had just finished filling up her car when she spotted her friend Alice across the garage forecourt. She put the hose back on the pump, and closed the fuel cap before waving over to Alice. Alice looked across, but ignored Helen. Thinking that she hadn't been seen, Helen waved again, only for Alice to appear to look, but ignore the wave.

Helen now shouted across the forecourt, "Oi, you silly tart, stop ignoring me."

Alice seemed shocked, and as Helen marched across to her, she understood why. It wasn't her friend Alice, but a total stranger.

"Sorry," Helen mumbled.

11th September

Willow

It's often said that I'm a bit of a diva, a prima donna if you will. I can see why people think that.

It's true that I prefer to eat only freshly prepared food, and that it's placed in exactly the right place before I'll eat it.

It's also true that I insist that people open doors for me, and I'll go through them without thanking them or closing it behind me.

I do like a comfortable warm place to sleep, and yes I do get easily spooked with loud noise.

But what do you expect, I'm only a cat.

12th September

I Don't Like Basil In My Soup

I looked suspiciously at the contents of my bowl. I was dubious about what appeared to be floating around in the soup. And it had the strangest taste to it, one I couldn't place. Eventually I had to ask the question.

"Hannibal old chap, what did you say this soup was again?"

"It's my unique new recipe tomato and chopped Basil."

"Are you sure? I can't taste any basil in it, and it appears to have some meaty bits in there."

"Yes that's right, the meaty bits would be Basil. Basil Spence. Surely you remember him from the rotary club."

13th September

A Carve Up

Jobu was one of hundreds of men abducted from Alaxis that were now forced to work on the travesty of a monument to the Emperor of Xefalis. All he did was carve symbols of power into the wood. He was shown which symbols had to go where and left to get on with it.

But Jobu had been reading in secret, learning what all the different symbols meant, and introducing subtle changes to them.

Today was the unveiling of the monument. The Emperor and his court were waiting for the shaman to power it up.

The explosion killed them all.

14th September

Alex Awake

Alex woke with a start, his hand hurt and when he looked it was caught in a mouse trap that did not have the cheese in it anymore.

There on his ironing board sat a jar of Nescafe and a dictionary opened at the first page. Freaked out he wandered to his bathroom and found thankfully that it was not masquerading as a Venus fly trap.

He took a deep breath and in doing so, the bee struck, stinging his tongue. Alex's mouth burned and, as he felt consciousness slipping away, his last thought was "should I cancel the milk?"

15th September

Short Cut

Too many times he'd given up on walking all the way around the estate back to his house, instead he'd clambered over the fence on Bedford Close, and through the little wooded glade before hauling himself over the wall into the back of his garden.

This time he'd struggled with the fence getting splinters embedded into his left hand, it was too dark for him to see them properly.

He knew he'd had too much to drink when he failed to get over his back wall.

He lay at the foot of the wall using the grass as a bed.

16th September

Pooh Sticks

He dropped the stick from the bridge into the water. He ran across the width of the bridge in time to see the stick come through the other side, and watched it float off.

Happy days for him.

Not so much for the stickleback the stick had landed on when dropped into the water, crushed to the bed of the stream, unable to swim anymore.

Not so much for the duck that was spooked on being hit by the stick downstream and flew into the electric fence.

And definitely not for the dog that drowned trying to retrieve the stick.

17th September

Drift Away

His mind wasn't on the meeting he was sat in. That much was hardly surprising, there was an on-going technical discussion about error messages being generated within the new system.

He didn't care, at the end of the day it wouldn't affect him, it wasn't going to be part of his role to look after the errors, and he wasn't in the payroll team anymore.

He was thinking about being at home, playing his records and enjoying the sound of music instead of people talking rubbish.

Suddenly he realised everyone was staring at him, they had asked him a question.

18th September

InsignificANT

It started with an ant.

Not a giant or an elephant, but a tiny ant, scurrying across the kitchen floor, dragging a leaf.

The cat and the dog spotted the leaf moving, but not the ant pulling it. They both dived for the leaf at the same time and became entangled.

The entanglement led to a fight, and all hell broke loose. They knocked the oven over, and the gas pipe ruptured.

The owner came and switched the light on to see what was happening.

Boom!

An ant scurried away from the burnt out shell pulling a leaf behind it.

19th September

Who Cares If It's Haunted?

They had tried to dissuade him from buying the house, telling him it was built over the top of an ancient cemetery. He had been told the house was haunted, and that was why it was so cheap. But he didn't care. He had been searching for this place for more than thirty years. He would have paid ten times the price they were asking for it if necessary.

He knew that buried underneath his new property was the grave of Eadwig, and that in that grave lay the long lost treasure of Eadwig. It was worth tens of millions.

20th September

Out Of The Shadows

It had been following her around all day. Every day. For the whole of her life. Sometimes it was behind her, occasionally it was in front of her, and at times it would be to one side of her or the other.

She had long become sick of its almost permanent presence in her life. But it wouldn't be around for much longer. Today was the day that all ended. Today was the day she was having the operation. She knew it was a controversial treatment, but she was going to have her shadow surgically removed.

21st September

Talent

Greg watched the girls win every event they entered, until they had run, jumped and thrown themselves out. They were now dragging him over for the parent's race.

It was the first family defeat of the day, and the girls asked him why he couldn't run faster? "I was never any good at sport; the two of you get all your talent from your dearly departed mother."

Greg hugged the girls, happy in the knowledge that they had Kristen very much a part of their being, and that he would always have her as long as the girls were around.

22nd September

Food Convoy

With six people heading for the restaurant, it would have to be a two car convoy.

However it didn't go to plan, they got stuck on the second traffic lights, slamming the brakes on when the lights turned to amber, but we were already through. There was nowhere for us to stop until the restaurant.

After fifteen minutes with no sign, I left the others at the restaurant and drove back home, where they were waiting.

"We got lost",

"Yes, we had gathered that, how about turning your mobile on?"

"We forgot about that, and we'd left it at home."

23rd September

Tattoo Time

It seemed like such a good idea at the time, well, being honest, what doesn't after a few drinks?

The four of them had decided it was a plan to go and get matching tattoos from the Zebub tattoo parlour down that dark alley in Lowtown. I mean, what could go wrong?

They weren't expecting the ink from their tattoos to start to spread and draw its own complex patterns all over their bodies. The ink formed summoning spells, and when they were covered head to toe in the arcane patterns it brought forth the Four Horsemen of the Apocalypse.

24th September

Quick Brown Fox

Whoever said "the quick brown fox jumps over the lazy dog" didn't live in our house.

As soon as the fox puts one foot in the back garden, the dog is up, barking like it's the apocalypse, running round the house knocking everything over, because it can't get traction on the laminate flooring.

The back door is opened and it is off and running. The fox squeezes back under the gate and the dog crashes face first into the fence trying to get it.

If the dog ever did catch the fox, it wouldn't know what to do with it.

25th September

The Ice

No one had ever found ice this deep beneath the surface of the planet. It was nearly two and a half miles deep under the formerly frozen tundra of Siberia. It should have been too warm for anything to be frozen that deep down.

When they got the samples back up to the surface and the makeshift town that had grown up there they were surprised when the ice didn't melt.

Instead when the seals were taken off, the ice evaporated, and the unseen, encased microbes escaped into the atmosphere, and in doing so The Human Race's fate was sealed.

26th September

Pecking

The bird was pecking away at something in the garden, and had been since before daylight. They had been trying to sleep through the pecking noise, trying to ignore it hoping it would go away. It hadn't been working.

Driven to distraction, they finally got out of bed and went downstairs to the garden to scare the bird off, but the bird ignored their shouts and kept pecking. Eventually he kicked it away, and they looked in amazement at what the bird had been pecking at.

There in the middle of their garden sat the tip of a buried coffin.

27th September

Failing Brakes

The brakes on Jas's van had failed, she was desperately trying to slow it down by down-shifting gears, but it wasn't really working. She swerved to avoid the parked bus and clipped a car in the opposite lane, then trying to correct the van's direction she over compensated. The van skidded and she mounted the pavement. The van hit at least one pedestrian before ploughing into the kebab shop.With the hard stop forced on the van, Jas hit her head on the steering wheel, and as she passed out her last thought was, "they will think I'm a terrorist."

28th September

Interrogation

He sat face to face with the two police officers across a wooden table, the tape recorder was running on the side. He'd refused a lawyer as he knew he hadn't done anything wrong.

"Do you know why you are here?" the officer asked.

"To answer your questions"

"So why aren't you giving us the answers we want?"

"Because I'm not a mind reader, how am I supposed to know what you want to hear?"

"Just tell us the truth."

"I am!"

"Well, we don't believe you."

"It's not my fault you're stupid."

"We're not!"

"You could have fooled me!"

29th September

Phone Problems

It was one of those days; she'd left her glasses at home and was struggling to see things on her desk properly. The various phones hadn't stopped ringing since the moment she had arrived that morning.

She needed to make a personal call herself and picked up her phone and started to dial the numbers required. Once she'd tapped the numbers in, she hit the red call button on the phone and held it up to her ear.

There was no ringing tone to be heard, then a colleague asked,

"Why have you got a calculator up to your ear?"

30th September

Meat Feast

Was the meat ever going to stop coming? For the last two hours an onslaught of meat had made its way to his table. Freshly cooked on spits, they brought it to you, heat haze radiating up from the spits as they carved slithers of meat from the spit skewer onto your plate. Pork sausages and gammon, fillet, rump, t-bone and philly cheese steak, chilli beef cubes, chilli coated chicken legs, roast chicken breast, minted lamb, swordfish, jumbo prawns, calamari, others he didn't recognise.

He finally flipped his card over to say no more.

Then walked home on four legs.

October

1st October

The Fog

It was one of those mornings where you couldn't see more than a few feet in front of you. It had been clear at first, but the hovering atmosphere of fog had now descended. It was so thick they were sure they were hitting it as they drove.

Driving at a snail's pace, with no idea where they were exactly, sat-nav had given up, and they were trying to see if they couldn't spot a road sign.

They saw a man walking along and stopped to ask him if he knew where they were.

"Sorry, I haven't got the foggiest!"

2nd October

The Nosy Hand Dryer

Someone had scratched the letter "I" out from the sticky label on the hand dryer. The message now read,

"This Hand Dryer Is Nosy".

It made me laugh when I noticed it as I was having that clandestine tryst.

What I came to find out was it was a more accurate description of the hand dryer than we realised. It was recording sound and vision all the time.

The tryst was caught on film, and it found its way onto YouTube and other social media channels. And I found my way out of my house and relationship.

Damn nosy dryer.

3rd October

Warning Lid

There I was, happily driving along, not a care in the world, when out of nowhere the hubby exclaims, "ooh, warning lid!"

I looked around expecting to see lots of lids flying towards us, but can't see a thing.

"What the hell do you mean, warning lid? Is this a warning about a danger zone for lids popping off jars and flying at people, or did you mean warning, there was a manhole cover lid missing that I might drive into?"

"I didn't say anything about a warning, I said Warninglid, it's the name of the village we're driving through."

4th October

Battle Plan

Henry had been trying to get an appointment in front of the committee for months. It had been a constant battle with the keeper of the diary to get in front of them to talk about his plan for a special re-enactment for the anniversary.

It was close now, it was already the fourth of the month and the anniversary was on the twenty-fifth.

She looked up at him, "I can squeeze you in at quarter past two tomorrow if that's OK?"

"Yes please", he replied eagerly.

There you are then Henry, the fifth at 14:15 in the Agincourt room.

5th October

Get A Notepad

He had stopped reading, turned his kindle off, turned the light off, and tried to go to sleep.

His mind wouldn't stop. He was having ideas for what to write for his next drabble. There were lots of strands, ideas about writing on subjects he knew about and was interested in.

Then he had a story flash into his mind and he counted the words in his head. He had about ninety, which was great he could work with that. He'd write it down when he got up in the morning.

The morning came.

If only he could've remember it!

6th October

Autumn Fall

A single leaf had started to change colour from green to yellow, was it really that time of year already?

The days passed quickly, and more colours came, reds and yellows, oranges and browns, then one by one the leaves came tumbling down.

A small front garden was fully in bloom, with hardy perennials' bright colours fighting off the gloom.

The wind came along and moved all the fallen leaves, and now the front garden can hardly be seen. Dead leaves causing death as they smother the flowers, blocking out the sun, and soaking up all the water from showers.

7th October

The Interview

Sitting there waiting for the interview to start.

Fully suited and booted and prepared as could be. Questions all rehearsed in my head. Researched the company, even thought of some questions that he could ask them.

The previous candidate filed out of the room, their face was a mask, impossible to read. Not a hint of whether they thought they had succeeded.

The telephone rang on the receptionist's desk, and I was told to make my way in.

I took my seat and my heart sank. No job here today, both my ex-wives were the interview panel, smiling like sharks.

8th October

Pigeon of Doom

The warlock fed the seed to his pigeon. He was the only warlock to have a pigeon as his familiar. The other warlocks of his guild ridiculed him over the fact he hadn't gotten himself a crow or a raven.

He didn't care what they thought at all.

A pigeon was much more in touch with his needs and his mind-set; it was much more subtle. When it came to the time for his reckoning, the human fodder in the kingdom would never see their end coming.

After all who would expect a pigeon to be the harbinger of doom?

9th October

Wrong Door

All of her life they had prepared her to perform the ritual. They had taught her the Ellandi language needed to perform the incantation; the sword play required and herb lore so she could make the ointments.

She had been chosen and trained to be the one to open the portal to hell. The whole village was gathered to see her bring about what they thought was their destiny.

But they had taught her too well; she knew the one word within the incantation to change to make it a portal utopia.

That was where she was going to go.

10th October

The Power Of Prayer

It seemed that my prayers had been answered, I opened my eyes, finding myself staring up at a mass of theatre billboards on Broadway, miles from the wilderness, somewhere I hadn't been before, but I recognised from countless films, it was somewhere I had always wanted to go, and now magically I was here.

A great wave of relief washed over me, it was the last emotion that I ever felt, the Mack truck whose horn had dragged me to my senses, pulling me to this place and time, hit me at forty miles an hour and killed me instantly.

11th October

Betrayal

The knights were being careful. They were watching out for an attack. It felt like an ambush spot to them. If one of their swords scraped the stone of the tunnel they were in, it would spark and ignite the gas that was down here.

They could only move slowly and in single file, it wouldn't take much to box them in, yet it was the only way they had left to them.

They needn't have worried about a spark or an enemy; one of their own, Garrimore, waited until they were all inside and threw in a flaming torch.

12th October

A Business Opportunity

Brighton Pavilion was built and Queen Victoria went to visit. She stopped overnight at The George Hotel. The owner rubbed his hands with glee. Frequent visits to Brighton meant regular overnight stays at his hotel.

He immediately went out and bought all the flowers on the market. He painted and decorated the rooms within an inch of their lives, spending every penny he had on it. If the Queen was going to stay here on a regular basis, the royal set would flock here too.

Only for the Queen to hate the Pavilion and vow never to go back again.

13th October

Webbing

The spiders had gone all out overnight it would seem. They really wanted to help with the authenticity of the house ready for Halloween.

There's a long string of fairy lights hanging around the hall that had never been taken down from the previous Christmas.

The spiders had been adding a whole host of threads around the existing cabling between each of the bulbs so that it now had the look of having a tube of webbing along the whole length.

The effect when the lights were turned on was great as the whole lot took on a blue hue.

14th October

Probe

She stared out of the cockpit window, awestruck by the brightness of the stars as she sped through space. Nothing seemed to be moving relative to her craft, despite the fact it was hurtling along at over 250,000 miles per hour.

It was slowing down from over ten times that speed as it came in to approach the moon of Cerebus. The deep space probe had indicated the moon had a breathable atmosphere, and that its gravity was ninety per-cent of the Earth's.

They touched down on the moon's surface and started to sink into the quicksand they'd landed in.

15th October

Time Machine

They'd finished work on the time machine, thousands of hours working out permutations for mass, volume, acceleration and time. They'd mapped co-ordinates for the trial journey, they were going to send a team member forward a day into an empty room next to their laboratory.

Hank, lead mathematician on the project had volunteered; he entered the chamber, watching the team program the details.

In a few seconds he would be next door tomorrow. The chamber blinked out of view and he found himself in the vacuum of space.

They had forgotten about the movement of the Earth around the Sun.

16th October

Amazon Wrapping

There was a knock on the door, it was a delivery man, with a huge box from Amazon.

She took the parcel, and it was very light for something that size, and she tried to remember what she had ordered.

She opened the big box and found lots of scrunched up brown paper. She removed all of this – enough to decorate a small room – and found a much smaller box inside.

She opened the second box and was greeted with lots of polystyrene balls. She tipped them out and almost missed the item she had ordered.

A pair of earrings.

17th October

Winning

“Hi, I’m here to claim my prize.”

“Your prize?”

“Yes, I’ve spent the last six weeks either just lying in bed or being sat in my armchair watching mindless rubbish on the TV. I haven’t been out anywhere, as per the guidance, and I haven’t done any exercise at all. Therefore, I’m here to claim a trophy as was stated in the government guidelines about what I’d get if I didn’t move very much at all.”

“It wasn’t a trophy you’d get, it was all one word, atrophy, muscle wasting that comes with lack of use.”

“So, no trophy then?”

18th October

The Village

He had been walking for a couple of hours when he came to a small village. It appeared to him as the bucolic picture perfect image of how an old English village should be.

As he stood on the green admiring the thatched cottages and the medieval church with its tower and spire; a group of people approached him.

"Hello there, we've been expecting you."

He was confused, why would anyone be expecting him here?

"You have? Who are you?"

"Yes, we’re the village council, and we’ve been expecting you for a while now, we ordered our idiot weeks ago."

19th October

Life On Mars

It was mid-afternoon, and the sky was a dark burnt orange colour, it was too early for night to be falling. It wasn't the normal overcast sense you got from heavy rain laden clouds. It was more like the kind of dusty orange glow that you associated with how the sky was portrayed in movies when action was taking place on Mars.

Everyone was transfixed by the strange colouration and wondered if it was an eclipse or even the end of the world, but it was just smoke from Iberian fires and North African dust, blown here by a storm.

20th October

The Talisman

The talisman around his neck was weighing him down, for such a small intricate piece of jewellery it was heavy beyond imagination.

It didn't fit over his head, and he had found no clasp to remove it, he had tried to break it, cut it, and melt it all to no avail, except causing himself pain, since the morning he had woken to find it around his neck.

He had kept it covered up since the encounter with the priest in Nessanville on the third day, being knelt before and proclaimed as the chosen one was a little bit unnerving.

21st October

Hide

The boy was hiding in the cupboard, he had seen the man who was looking for him before, but his confused young brain couldn't tell him when or where.

The man was calling the boy's name, how did this man know his name? He could hear the voice getting closer, it was close enough for him to hear footsteps in the room now.

The steps came across the room and stopped outside the cupboard. The door was flung open and the light flooded in. His mother stood there frowning at him,

"Stop being silly Timmy, say hello to your uncle."

22nd October

That Wasn't Quite What We Asked For

Will it work I could hear them all say. Ever since I had announced that I had a panacea for all the problems on the planet there had been a buzz about what it would be. What was it that could possibly solve war, hunger, poverty, disease and more all in one go?

As I addressed the world by video link from my secret location I laid out the plan to put an end to all the problems of the world. The countdown to it being released was now on.

My planet splitting bomb would wipe it all out.

BOOM!

23rd October

Darkness

She lay in her bed staring into the darkness in her room, a small sliver of murky light was coming in around the edges of the blackout blind, but it wasn't enough to stop her enjoyment of the dark.

There was something moving around in the room, trying to be quiet, but struggling with the darkness, and therefore bumping into things.

Whatever it was probably thought it would be able to scare her, to make her cry out in the dark, but they would be wrong, she was the queen of the dark, and she was going to scare them.

24th October

Incredulous

They had enjoyed the show, and had left the theatre to go and get some food in Chinatown. They found the little restaurant in the side street, that they had made reservations at a few days before.

They were shown to their seats and given menus to browse through, the pair of them taking a few minutes to make their choices, and the waiter took their order.

"… and some special fried rice please."

"Sorry, we don't have any rice."

They couldn't believe what they had heard, how was it possible for a Chinese restaurant not to have any rice?

25th October

A Monster

The monster whooshed down out of the sky and landed with a roar in a cloud of dust next to where he had been sleeping on the bench. The roar had woken him from his stupor, and he struggled to work out where he was. He saw the monster shaking in front of his eyes and tried to move back from it only to find the bench's back prevented him from doing so.

He tried to work out what the creature was: only recognising it as the dust cleared. It was a gargoyle, fallen from the roof of the church.

26th October

Knob Polishing

She saw the old man raise his eyebrows, she knew what was coming.

"It says here, your previous job was a knob polisher, what did that entail?"

There was a lascivious look on his face, but he was going to be disappointed.

"Have you been to look around Arundel Castle?"

"Yes."

"Did you see how many doors there were?"

"Yes."

"Well, I had to polish each of the seven hundred and fourteen door knobs every day."

The gleam went out of his eyes.

"So, it's not a euphemism then?"

"No it isn't you dirty old man, I'm just a cleaner."

27th October

On The Run

He'd been on the run for three weeks now, just managing to avoid their clutches on several occasions. He didn't understand how they kept finding him, he'd dumped all of his old clothes, and picked up new ones in charity shops. He hadn't used any of his bank cards since drawing out thousands in the first couple of days, and he'd dismantled and disposed of his phone. He hadn't used his own name in all that time either, yet still they came, homing in on him unerringly.

Being eight foot tall and green was a bit of a giveaway though.

28th October

MPB

She turned around and looked at the row of four people sat at their desks behind her and she laughed.

All four of them were male, and were lined up in age order, each of them a little bit greyer and a little bit balder than the man to their right.

She couldn't help herself, as she giggled to herself, she moved to a place where she could get them all into the same picture and happily took the snap.

Straight into Twitter to post the picture with the caption "The four ages of male pattern balding."

It went viral.

29th October

Carving

They were carving faces into pumpkins; not just pumpkins, but other types of squashes as well. Different faces carved in to different sizes, shapes and colours of vegetables.

They were all done apart from one type of squash. They were undecided as to what face to carve into it. I decided to throw in one of my typically unhelpful.

"Why don't you do a horse's face on that one?"

Blank looks followed, they wanted me to explain.

"Well it's long, and they always say "A Horse walked into a bar and was asked, why the long face?""

Groans all around.

30th October

Spider

He had woken up that morning and could see something out of the corner of his eye. When he tried to concentrate on what it was it seemed to move out of focus and slip away from him.

It seemed like it was the legs of a spider, slowing moving its legs around, and it felt itchy as hell. He had rubbed his eyes, but it seemed to have split the vision up and there was now more in the corner of his eye.

He looked in the mirror and saw the problem. There WAS a spider in his eye.

31st October

Halloween

He loved Halloween, the people wandering around in fancy dress, whether scary or surprising. There really was no limit to what some parents would dress their kids like.

He walked past a group of parents and children as they were trick-o-treating. All of the group looked over at him, and he drew a number of comments.

“Awesome costume man!”

“That blood splatter looks great, and so realistic.”

“Cool knife bro!”

He loved Halloween, no need for him to get changed after his latest murder, he could wander the streets covered in his victim’s blood and no one batted an eyelid.

November

1st November

Bonfire

Late October and once again they were building the official bonfire for the fireworks extravaganza. He didn't know why they bothered to build it before the day, every year someone got in the night before and burnt it down, and they would have to work like lunatics to rebuild the fire again.

They had tried guards, dogs, CCTV and booby traps but nothing had worked, when it got to the fourth of November someone sneaked in and set it alight. He had a plan to prevent that this year.

Whilst dressed as Frankenstein on Halloween, he burnt it down himself.

2nd November

Three Letter Hero

Too far, too old, one owl, one toe, one hop.

Low pig sty mud, red mud, was wet and old, but dry now, sun out.

Can you see how she can see all she can see?

Out one eye o'er her lid, too far o'er sea and sun.

Her ear can aid you, her arm can ail you, her leg can end you, her lip can rub you.

All you see, all you are, all you can get, has now put its all for her.

You can not end her, she has all the day and eve, she has won.

3rd November

Furniture

He looked out of his twenty-seventh story window down over the cityscape below him.

He knew that what he had done over the course of his career to get him to this office with a view will have affected many of the people who were out walking those streets, working in those buildings, or living in those houses.

Not for much longer though, he was retiring, he was getting too old to have to deal with this anymore, it was a younger man's game.

He would miss it, but it was someone else's turn to be the DFS sale scheduler.

4th November

Swimming

She'd always liked swimming, some of her earliest memories had been of swimming. In the pool on holiday, in the sea, at the local swimming baths; she never felt happier than when she was in the water, alone with her thoughts as she swam, back and forth, arms and legs working in unison to propel her through the water.

She didn't like this water she was in though. The river was running high and fast, her clothes were soaked and dragging her down; her strength was failing.

She had saved her little terrier, Sooty, now she had to save herself.

5th November

Build A Bonfire

She had sneaked back and forth to the bonfire many times the previous night, carefully depositing the items into the solid stack that had been built to accompany the firework display tonight.

She stood carefully watching the bonfire as they went to light it, praying they wouldn't stop and pull out any of the items she had spent ages hiding in there.

The fire was lit and took quickly, roaring away, with small flakes floating off from it. He husband seemed to enjoy it, blissfully unaware that the fire was being given extra impetus by all his old fishing magazines.

6th November

The Joy Of Fireworks

It was that time of year for fireworks, when the setting off of them seemed to happen every night from early October through to a week after Bonfire Night. With Diwali and Halloween in that period it just seemed like it was any excuse to let off some fireworks.

However the pets don't like it, there is cowering in the bath tub. Then managing to find a way through to the back of the bookcase where they can't get back out.

When the fireworks stop there is the clean-up, dog poo in the bath and cat wee behind the bookcase.

7th November

The Hole

The earthquake had opened up a hole in the rock face. They shone their torches into the blackness and although the light flicked across top, bottom and sides to the hole, the light couldn't penetrate through the darkness to the back of the hole.

They decided to enter the hole and explore where it went. Shining the torches ahead of them as they walked they followed the route that the passageway inside the hole took them.

For over two hours they followed its meandering route through the dark until a door appeared.

"Enter!" boomed a voice on the other side.

8th November

The Case

The phone rang on the detective's desk, a shrill noise invading the silence. She let it ring three times before answering, drawling the words "Malone Private Eye".

Heavy breathing came over the line before a gravelly voice said, "I've got a case for you."

Without wanting to sound eager, she eventually replied, "How do you know I'll want it?"

"It's got your name all over it."

"Where?"

"In the lobby, I can't make it up the steps."

She hung up and went to the lobby. There it was; a big green suitcase with her name in big letters on it.

9th November

Opening The Case

“This is your case then?” the voice was no less gravelly in person.

“So it says.”

“Sign here then please.”

She did, and he left. She took the case from the lobby, back up to her office, perspiring as she dragged it up the stairs. They really needed to fix the lift. She heaved the case up onto her desk and looked for how to open it. There was a big clasp on the side, which flipped up. The case opened a small bit, stopping to show a key hole.

It was at the moment, an open and shut case.

10th November

A Strange Present

She went to her equipment locker and pulled out the bolt cutter, bringing them back to her desk and the case. She used the bolt cutters to break the lock, it giving more easily than she had expected. She put the bolt cutters down on her chair and fully opened the case.

Inside, behind each of the zipped dividers sat nothing but cricket balls, hundreds of the heavy red balls; no wonder the case was so damn heavy.

A note was pinned to the inner divider.

“To the only maiden for me, hopefully all of these will bowl you over.”

11th November

Finding A Clue

She'd no idea whose affection she was receiving, but surely there had to be a better way of expressing it, other than a couple of hundred cricket balls.

She looked at the note again, looking for signs of where it had come from. The paper wasn't watermarked, or from a branded pad, but she could see indentations from words written on sheets above this one.

She got out her dusting kit, and traced the previous message. The handwriting was the same, the note saying.

"The Shard, viewing gallery, midday Thursday."

Only an hour away, it would be a high noon.

12th November

Solved

She ran down the stairs and out of the lobby, into the street to flag down a taxi, heading for the Shard. She sneaked in through a service entrance and got in to a lift.

She almost left her stomach behind as it shot up, and as the doors opened she lurched into the viewing gallery.

It was deserted except for the voice behind her. "Very good Bugsy."

She hated that name, she turned and there was her childhood sweetheart Kenneth.

"You could have just called me for a DATE!"

"Yes, but it's always best if you FIGure it out."

13th November

Headache

There was a dull throb in the middle of his forehead, just above the eyes, and it was annoying him. He'd tried drinking lots of water, taking paracetamol and lying in a darkened room, but none of them had seemed to work, the dull throb remained.

It felt like there was a little person on the inside, bashing on his skull to get out.

He didn't know how close to the truth that was until the front of his head exploded outwards and a horde of little creatures poured out of the hole and down his face as he collapsed.

14th November

Rodizio

Everyone had ordered the Rodizio, the never ending supply of meats on skewers. There was a whole array of other food, vegetables, salad, fried items and cold meats and cheese on the buffet, but why waste room on that stuff when the freshly cooked meats kept appearing at the table.

Different cuts of steak, Brazilian sausage, lamb, spicy chicken, chilli beef, carved off the skewer at our table. Then the cinnamon coated grilled pineapple

There would definitely be food comas all round when we got home.

Apart from Granville, he was already quite happily fast asleep at the table already.

15th November

E-Mail Hell

The last e-mail had pushed him over the edge.

He picked up his keyboard and used it like a baseball bat, swinging at anything and everything in range, screens, phones, people, nothing was safe.

A few keys fell out, and he picked them up and started eating them.

He then ran as fast as he could and flung himself at the window. He bounced back. He tried another three times with the same result, but finally managed to break through the glass and fall on the fifth attempt.

The suicide attempt failed, he forgot he worked on the ground floor.

16th November

The Substitute

I sat on the substitutes' bench, more nervous than I'd ever been in my long and successful life. Time was ticking down, both in the game and on my life.

I was told to warm up, not easy for an overweight septuagenarian, and then the board went up in the 89th minute and I was going to make my Premier League debut. I had dreamt of this moment since I was a child, but never thought it could happen.

Then I had a lot of good fortune and I made it happen. It's helps of course, to own the club.

17th November

Cinema Visit

It was that time of year again, the time for their annual trip to the cinema, a fraught time where lots of money was spent on overly expensive tickets, to sit in seats that were uncomfortable and covered with various dubious substances. Then there was all the other extra money, drinks, sweets, popcorn, all costing enough to put a third world country into budget deficit.

Then there would be the moaning, the problems encountered when the expensive food and drink ended up on the floor, followed by the tears and the tantrums.

Stop it Ted, you're a fully grown man!

18th November

The Cat Is Fast

Today at the Grand Prix of Catalonia, history was made as Sniffles the cat became the first ever feline winner of a grand prix, or any other motor race for that matter. (And to be fair the first ever non-human winner of any such race either.) We can now go over to the Barcelona track for a live interview with the extraordinary winner of the race.

"Hello Sniffles, many congratulations on you being the first ever feline Grand Prix winner after such an amazing drive. Could you tell all our viewers how you managed to win the race today?"

"Meeeeeoooooaaaaawwwwww."

19th November

Boots

I woke up to the words "And one of these days these boots are going to walk all over you!" I struggled to get my bearings as I opened my eyes and tried to figure out where I was.

The last thing I remember was being in the bar doing shots of tequila, we were due to be going on to a club.

By the sounds of it, it was some kind of fetish club.

But these were my sheets, and my pillowcases, it was my room.

The words had music attached, it was my damn alarm, time for work.

20th November

Do You Deliver?

I'm sat in the pub, and I'm watching Deliveroo drivers coming in out. And I'm wondering who the cheeky feckers are who are ordering food in to be delivered to the pub. It took the third Deliveroo driver coming in before I realised they weren't delivering food to people in the pub, they are picking up takeaways orders from the pub to deliver out to people sat in their nice warm homes.

This is after drink one. My brain thinks that this could get messy already.

Then it gets to 1am and the Dominos delivery turned up to the pub.

21st November

Move Your Car

"Why didn't you use the front pump, instead of this back one, blocking me from using it?"
"I rolled my eyes and sighed, "When I got here, there was something parked in front of me."
"Why didn't you move down when they left?"
"Because I was inside paying, and as yet, the technology to enable me to be in two places at once doesn't exist."
"Just move your car."
"I will, when I'm ready, if you're too much of an impatient halfwit to wait for that, move to a row where there are spaces. Which looking, is any of them."

22nd November

The Conversation

"Hi, is Kev in?"
"Fay, Is Kev in?"
"No he isn't, who's calling?"
"No, he's not in."
"Do you know where he's gone?"
"Fay, where's he gone?"
"I don't know, who is on the phone?"
"No, I don't know where he's gone."
"Do you know when he'll be back?"
"Fay, what time will he be back?"
"I don't know Tom, ask who it is."
"No I don't know what time he'll be back. Who is it calling?"
"It's Karl."
"Hi Karl, how are you doing? He's gone to The Owl And The Pussycat, he'll be back about half past nine."

23rd November

Tell Us A Joke

There I am, sat minding my own business at Manchester Victoria when two scallies approach.

"Hey look it's Johnny Vegas, hey Johnny, tell us a joke."

"I'm not Johnny Vegas."

"Yeah you are, where's Monkey?"

"How the hell would I know, I'm not Johnny Vegas."

"Yes you are, go on, tell us a joke."

"If I tell you a joke, do you promise to do one?"

"Yeah mate."

"Ok then, what's the best position to have sex in if you want to have really ugly children?"

"Dunno mate, what position?"

"Go and ask your parents."

"Ha, ha, good one mate."

24th November

Drains

The kitchen sink was blocked, water had pooled back into the sink, and wasn't going down, the wire brush had been poked down as far as possible and had only brought up black gunge. Attempts to use a plunger weren't helping as the air was coming of the overflow.

They managed to block the overflow and retried the plunger and there was movement, the water began to subside a little, so repeated use of the plunger followed, more movement, but a smell came from the washing machine, she opened the door just as he plunged and got covered in gunge.

25th November

Get A Hat

If you want to get ahead then get a hat. The saying is used in the classic game "The Secret of Monkey Island", where a leaflet headed with it was used to persuade the cannibals to let the hero Guybrush Threepwood have their enchanted head.

Over the years I have followed this saying quite religiously, in addition to accumulating enough headwear to wear a different hat every day for a month, I can't help putting anything remotely hat like on my head.

If only I had a pound for each time I've heard "Take that lampshade off of your head."

26th November

A Deadly Kiss

She loved the bright, vibrant red lipstick that her husband bought her and wore it every day. The shade was called vermilion, but she didn't know it contained cinnabar, actual vermilion, until she started to fall ill. By the time she saw a doctor and had tests it was too late to stop the mercury poisoning from killing her.

But her husband wasn't getting away with killing her. She had taken another of the lipsticks he had bought her and had crushed bits of it into his food, the heat and colour of his favourite curries hiding it from him.

27th November

Food Advice

A Mars a day helps you work, rest and play.

An apple a day keeps the doctor away.

Berocca, you, but on a really good day.

Counts as one or two of your five a day.

Advertising advice flooding the mind, eat healthy or eat junk, just take their product and get it down your neck. But I don't want to, if I want a bun, with a double burger, with triple cheese, and four bottles of cola, then that's what I'll have.

Granted, I'll also have high cholesterol, high blood pressure and diabetes, but I'll be happy and full.

28th November

Drink Me

The drinks were laughing at her, she was sure of it. They were all having a good giggle, conspiring, making fun of her. She desperately wanted to drink them all and they knew it. The glasses of wine, the rum and coke, the vodka, lime and soda, even the Sambuca shots and jagerbombs.

They were all taunting her and her glass of orange juice and lemonade. Slip a gin into it they whispered.

But she couldn't, they would all have to wait until another night. She would stick to her soft drinks; after all she was the night's designated driver.

29th November

Surprise Delivery

A knock on the door in the middle of the night was a surprise. It probably wouldn't even have woken me up if it hadn't set the dog off on one of his barking frenzies.

I went down the stairs to the front door, managing to shove the dog into the living room. At the door was a delivery driver, his van parked blocking the road in the middle of the cul-de-sac, lights on and music blaring.

"What the hell are you doing delivering at this time of night?"

"I was passing on my way back home from the club."

30th November

Anyone Else?

"It's St Andrews day, it's a great day to be Scottish." "Or Greek for that matter." "Yes, or Greek I suppose." "Russian and Ukrainians as well." "Yes them too." "Don't forget Barbados, they have him as well." "OK."

"The Georgians do too." "Really, surely they would have St George with that name?" "They do, but they have St Andrew as well, same as Romania." "Anyone else?" "Yeah, Sicilians, some Maltese, some Italians and the Cypriots."

"Jeez, is there anyone who isn't celebrating St Andrew today?"

"The more the merrier I say, just as long as it's not the damn English!"

December

1st December

What Corruption?

“Yes!”

“Yes what mate?”

“I’ve just had it confirmed that we have managed to get that contract to do all the new anti-fraud and anti-bribery training courses for that multi-national power company.”

“How did we manage that, they weren’t keen on our training packages, and I thought we’d been undercut by at least two of the other companies that had put together RFI’s.”

“That’s true, but I had a bit of a brainwave.”

“You did? Why what did you come up with.”

“Well, after being told we’d been undercut by twenty grand, we bunged them a twenty five grand kickback.”

2nd December

Licky Licky

He woke to his face being licked and no recollection as to where he was. If he was at home then there was a strong likelihood that the damn dog had got in to the bedroom and was licking his face.

He struggled to open his eyes, but as he did he didn’t recognise what he saw. The camouflage netting hanging across the ceiling suggested that he wasn’t at home. He really didn’t know where he was.

When he turned his head to see what was licking him, he certainly wasn’t prepared to come face to face with a goat.

3rd December

Record Hunt

He had been in the record store for at least three hours, he had flicked through every record in every rack apart from the one he was currently on. He'd found a few items he would buy, but on the whole had been disappointed with what was around in the shop this time.

Then he saw it, he'd nearly flicked straight past it as his will to keep hunting was waning. He went back a couple of records and pulled it out of the rack.

It was what he'd been hoping to find.

In mint condition.

Gary Glitter's Greatest Hits.

4th December

Moving Dance Floor

It wasn't the first time that he had been to a disco on a boat. The last time he had, at least the boat had been docked at the time. That particular boat had had at least half a dozen different dance floors, and the one that rotated was supposed to move.

The dance floor on this boat wasn't moving, it just felt like it was. There was a clear and present danger of him falling over.

He needed the DJ to play "Oops upside your head", at least that way there was an excuse to sit on the floor.

5th December

Now Listen Up

She shouted out in frustration, her earphones had disappeared off the side again. The damn lodger had no concept of personal items or even ownership, he was forever taking items that were not his and using them in such a way that no one else would want to touch them again afterwards.

She went to retrieve her earphones. He was lying on the bed, with the pods in his ears and his eyes closed.

She would need new headphones yet again, but the lodger would not be taking them in the future. She had strangled him with the last set.

6th December

Declined

“Card declined”, repeated the assistant reading from the card machine.

The woman looked shocked, waving her card around as the assistant gave her the confirmation receipt from the machine. The woman paused briefly before speaking again.

“I have a theory as to why that card has been declined, would it be possible to split the transaction into two amounts?”

The assistant sighed, saying, “Only if we split it into two different transactions, for which I’d need to rescan all the items.”

Someone from the back of the queue shouted.

“I have a theory as well. You don’t have enough money!”

7th December

Ideas

The pen sped across the page as she tried to get all the ideas out of her head down on paper to refer to later, knowing full well she wouldn't remember half of it when it really mattered.

So quickly the pen moved it wasn't leaving ink so much, as scorch marks on the page. And then it stopped, the ideas having come to an end, nothing more flowed from the pen.

She took a breath and looked at the page below, and cried.

There were no words on the page at all.

The pen still had its lid on.

8th December

Water Butt

Two Irishmen turn up with a freshly creosoted water butt. "We've got this butt for Tom." It was six foot tall and four foot in diameter, and wouldn't fit down the entry.

"We could throw a rope over the house and pull it over." Fay looked at them in disbelief. The small guy scratched his head under his cap and creosote ran down his face.

"How about we pass it across all the back gardens?" "No!"

"Remove the doors and take it through the house." "No!"

Tom makes an appearance and they decide to take it to the allotment instead.

9th December

Shoes Only

The queue for the entrance to the bar was ridiculous, snaking up the road. As they got closer they heard the words, "Shoes only," but they had trainers on and after queuing didn't want to be turned away.

They took their trainers off and stuck them in their back pockets, one in each, and approached the door in just socks.

They got past the first bouncer, but then they noticed the trainers in their pockets, and they were rumbled that they were just in socks.

Five minutes later, trainers on, but with socks over the top they sail in.

Result.

10th December

Death Comes To Call

The lights flickered. The cats both woke as if scalded and they fled from the room. The dog's hackles rose and he growled at the door. The temperature in the room dropped and it was possible to see the dog's breath float into the room as he continued to growl.

Then the lights flickered for a second time and I got up to leave the room, feeling lighter than I ever had before. I found myself joining hands with Death as I did so.

The dog stopped growling and I turned to see him licking my body's cold dead hand.

11th December

I Can't Believe You Used A Butter Knife

Pictures emerged of an armed robber at the garage. He was wearing three hats and purple washing up gloves. He was armed with a knife, though pictures showed it was a butter knife, and he fled empty handed.
"Give me all the money."
"No."
"I've got a knife."
"So?"
"If you don't hand over all the money I'll spread this butter all over you!"
"Is it salted butter?"
"What?"
"Is it salted butter?"
"erm, no, it's some kind of margarine."
"Do you worst then, I'm only allergic to salt."
"Do you sell salted butter?"
"No."
"I'll be back later then."

12th December

I Don't Like Sweet Things

"So then Ciaran, would you like some dessert? There's a chocolate fudge cake in the fridge, or there is apple strudel in the freezer."

"Erm, no, it's OK, I don't really like sweet things thanks."

And then not more than five minutes later as I sat at the kitchen table, Ciaran came back into the kitchen and started rummaging through the cupboard to get to the chocolate bourbons. He took a few of them to have with his coffee. Then a couple of minutes after that he came back and took some more.

So glad we bought those savoury bourbons.

13th December

One Hundred Years On

It is the third of September 2039. Russia has just invaded Poland after telling anyone who would listen that they had no expansion plans.

Londonia unfriends Russia on TwitFace. The strongest condemnation a country is now allowed to give openly.

Only minutes after the unfriending, Londonia's account is then hacked to post the message;

"Lolz polish them off."

Nobody laughs, nobody hits like, lots of nations unfriend Londonia, despite pleas of innocence.

One nation dies. One nation moans about the spelling involved. TwitFace suspend Londonia. No one else dares to unfriend Russia.

Emperor Trump mocks them all from his spaceship.

14th December

The Atlas

The old man always carried the battered old book around wherever he went. It looked as if it was only being held together by luck and will. When asked about it, he always told people that it is the good book he likes to get lost in.

Alone in his room the old man locked the door and opened the atlas. He picked a map at random from the well-thumbed pages, placed his finger on the page at a spot on the land and he said the incantation.

And then he was gone, perhaps he would get lost this time.

15th December

Caught

The young boy went to the normal place in the shop and picked up a handful of packs of stickers, he would stick them in his pockets as normal and walk out after getting the paper for his parents.

There was a slight wrinkle in the plan, the trousers he wore had no pockets and the shopkeeper caught him trying to hide the stickers under his top.

His mum found out the next day. He was banned from collecting stickers for years, and she made him go out with a sign around his neck that said,

“I am a thief.”

16th December

Scratch

The scratching at the door was a constant echo in the back of her mind, was she still dreaming of something, or was she awake and there was something at the door?

She opened her eyes and the noise continued. It was annoying her now. She got out of bed and went to the bedroom door where the noise was coming from, and opened it.

There was nothing there. The noise stopped, and she closed the door and went back to bed.

She closed her eyes and the scratching started again.

This time it was in the bed with her.

17th December

Sunset

The sun had set beyond the horizon, and was lighting up the sky in the most wonderful way. Deep terracotta orange at the base, lightening to yellow, before transitioning into a cavalcade of blue, with white tips on the few wispy clouds that gently floated in the sky.

The rooftops that could be seen out of the window blended in with the bare tree branches in a silhouette of black lining the sky's kaleidoscope of colours.

I was transfixed by the view as it slowly changed.

Then someone turned the lights on and all I could see was my reflection.

18th December

Hangover

He opened his eyes, and quickly shut them again, his head throbbed and his mouth felt like someone had sandpapered it.

He felt nauseous, and his body felt like stone, especially his legs. He hadn't had a hangover like this for as long as he could remember.

How much did he have to drink last night? He was fine on the pints, but those shots and the champagne finished him off. He could just about recollect crawling over the doorstep and up the stairs into bed.

His wife came in and said. "The pub rang, you left your wheelchair there."

19th December

The End Of Time

She never heard the captain draw his sword, the first she knew was when she found herself looking up at her body sat in the chair from the vantage point of the floor where her head landed.

The captain was pouring fuel over her head and body and she found herself unable to speak or to stop what was happening. The flames took hold of her searing her skin from her frame and reducing her to ash. It didn't hurt as she expected it to; she just felt her spirit leaving her charred remains.

She was a vampire no more.

20th December

Secret Santa

"DIY Made Easy" was the title of the book.

Someone who obviously didn't know him well had given it to him in secret Santa. DIM would be more appropriate – destroy it myself – was the outcome of any home improvements.

Clumsy was an understatement.

The bookcase had a missing shelf, where he'd stood on it whilst unpacking it from the flatpack.

The chair was missing an arm from resting laminate flooring on it to cut to size. Cut through the arm perfectly, but the floor panel was wonky.

Perhaps the sender did know him, and was actually plotting to kill him!

21st December

Can You Swim?

A Christmas party being held on a boat as it eased its way up and down the River Thames in the dark of the night was different. The fact that there would be a plethora of people on the boat that annoyed the hell out of him all year was an opportunity.

He wondered how many of the others at the party could swim. There was a real possibility that some may accidentally meet the water of the Thames in the dark.

Did they have enough lifejackets?

Man overboard indeed, and just for good measure, a number of women too.

22nd December

The Christmas Party

It's the work Christmas party tonight, for once let someone else be the star of the show, let someone else make a fool of themselves, it doesn't have to be you.

The meal is poor as always, you'd have been better off with burger and chips, but now the wine is flowing, there's always bottles of red left over.

It's that time of the night, glasses are dispensed with, drinking straight from the bottle.

Pass out in the corner and end up getting decorated with anything on hand by your colleagues.

At least you didn't moon the boss this year.

23rd December

Tipping Point

He had drink number three in front of him, this was the tipping point, between getting home today and being able to participate in the family get together tomorrow, or stumbling around at 4am, with remnants of kebab all over his clothes, wondering if he was going to make it home.

It would take him less than five minutes to finish off the pint and then it was decision time.

The time ticked by, another drink or home. Home or another drink. He thought about the family get together again, and realised the right thing to do.

Same again please.

24th December

Another Christmas Eve

Another Christmas Eve, following the pattern established over the last few years; out early in the evening, around the local pubs, lots of drinks and all round frivolity. Then at closing time, make the journey over to the local church for midnight mass. Twenty drunken friends, who never go to church, making their annual pilgrimage to Our Lady's, some still with tinsel on their heads.

They crowd into rows near the back, some even go for communion instead of a kebab. The priest doesn't care, he's half cut too.

Then back home just in time for The Italian Job again.

25th December

Santa's Been

"Daddy, daddy, wake up, Santa's been."

I wearily opened my eyes, it was only six in the morning, Santa hadn't been, it was us, up at three in the morning, the kids had eventually fallen asleep, waiting for Santa.

As I got up I felt the acid reflux, having a mince pie and glass of sherry at stupid o'clock in the morning hadn't been a great idea.

We went downstairs to the meagre amount of presents that were there for the kids, it had been a tough year.

But no, there were lots of huge presents, Santa really had been.

26th December

Inevitable

I woke up normally this morning; there were no over-excited kids jumping on the bed; ready to see if Santa had been.

The previous day's food and drink is making movement difficult this morning, yet it's likely to be more of the same today. We're off round to the in-laws for dinner and polite conversation, but at least today there is some sport on, football and racing, the bookies is open, and there's time for a stop in the pub.

Some have gone shopping, the sales have started. Then I hear a distant boom. My credit card has just exploded.

27th December

They Are Everywhere

It had been painstaking work. The cursive script made the document almost impossible to read he didn't understand why it hadn't been digitalised at the time it was written, everything else from the time was apart from all the deeds.

And now he had finally deciphered the documents and knew the answer the colonists of Gemini V had been trying to find for millennia.

Who had given the go ahead and license for a Maccy D's to be opened on their new planet?

He would be hung, drawn, and quartered when the planet's populace found out it was his relatives.

28th December

Ready To Write

He sat up in bed, trying to think of something to write, he had the notepad and the pen primed, ready for action. Many was the time that the ideas had flowed as he lay in bed, but no pen or paper had been to hand, and by the morning the ideas had gone, drifted away over night to that writing idea heaven that snaffled so many of his great ideas over the years.

The pen was poised over the page waiting for that idea to come, itching to lay down ink on the white paper below.

Yet nothing came.

29th December

Sound

In the three minutes the song had been playing, the record had revolved 100 times. 100 times that little fleck of dust had passed under the arm, and then it was caught by the needle.

It was trapped there, and as the vinyl moved beneath it, the dust stayed stuck to the needle, being dragged through the groove, feeling every little contour within it as the needle picked up the changes and sent them on.

Then the needle lifted from the groove, and the owner removed the dust from it, and dropped it to the floor.

Then the song continued.

30th December

Tricky Ending

He'd been slavishly working on his first book for months now. Every spare moment he got out of work he was tapping away on his laptop. The story he had ended up with was a long way from the one he had set out to write, but the ending to the story was impossibly hard to write.

He put the laptop down on the bannister to close the door behind him, and then turned and watched in horror as he knocked it off, and saw it bounce down the stairs.

Definitely not the ending he was looking for at all.

31st December

Entry Fee

“What do you mean it’s thirty pounds to get in?”

“New Year’s Eve mate, special entry price for the entertainment.”

“You’ve entertainment every other Saturday night, and it’s free to get in, who have you got booked this time? The Rolling Stones?”

“No, one of the normal acts, but everything costs more on New Year’s Eve.”

“Is there food and drink included?”

“No, you still need to pay for that.”

“So apart from an act I can see for free normally, what else is included in the price?”

“Nothing.”

“How many people have you had in then?”

“None so far.”

How this book came to be written

Hello to all the readers who have made it this far. I hope you enjoyed this collection of drabbles. Some of you may be asking, Why drabbles?

Well, I fell into writing by accident. I hadn't realised how much I wrote when I lived in Manchester, I was in too much of an alcoholic haze at the time to know just how much I had done.

Then in 2016 I was getting a daily e-mail from the (now on hiatus) BookHippo website, and at the end of each e-mail there was a drabble, a hundred-word story, and there was an open invitation for readers of the e-mail to submit their own drabbles. I tried sending a couple of them in towards the end of November 2016 and the very first one I sent was published in the e-mail and on their website (Inanimate – February 12th in this collection). For the next year I would regularly send more in, I ended up sending over a hundred in, and seventy-three of them were published before the website went on hiatus.

At the same time I was writing additional drabbles, trying to write one a day for a year, which I completed before the end of 2017. And then I didn't write one for a couple of years, but I do now write them on occasions, and average about one a month.

That initial blast of writing drabbles, and getting the feedback from them being published on that website encouraged me to dig out my Manchester writing from fifteen years before, which I still had all copies of on e-mails and on an old website I had put together. Part of that was an ongoing story from which I pulled a book together, revised and edited it several times and have finally gotten around to publishing that this year as well.

Since then I have joined several writing groups, completed another three novels which I am querying, and had poetry and short stories published in various collections.

And all from doing that a little one-hundred-word story. One of my other completed novels, which I am currently querying came from a drabble I did. The book of The Talisman (October 20th in this collection) ended up being over one hundred thousand words long.

<u>About the author</u>

Kev Neylon is a writer who lives with his partner Helen in Crawley in West Sussex. When he is not writing fiction, he is writing blog posts about his travels, or on the history of Leicester and Crawley, or match reports on the Crawley Town games he attends as a season ticket holder.

To keep up to date with what else he has published, and access to his blog and other social media channels, follow him on one or more of the below.

Website: - https://www.onetruekev.co.uk/
Twitter: - @onetruekev
Instagram: - @onetruekev
Facebook: - https://www.facebook.com/Onetruekev/
Medium: - https://onetruekev.medium.com/
LinkedIn: - https://www.linkedin.com/in/onetruekev/

Also available is his debut novel;

Where The Lights Shine Brightest.

Get it as a paperback or eBook available on Amazon.

Printed in Great Britain
by Amazon

41572200R00116